EYE OF ATHINA

ROGER W THOMPSON

2QT LIMITED (PUBLISHING)

First Edition published 2011 by
2QT Limited (Publishing)
Dalton Lane, Burton In Kendal
Cumbria LA6 1NJ
www.2qt.co.uk

Cover Design by Robbie Associates Ltd
Cover Images supplied by Shutterstock Images LLC

Printed in Great Britain by
the MPG Books Group, Bodmin and King's Lynn

Mixed Sources

Product group from well-managed
forests, controlled sources and
recycled wood or fiber
www.fsc.org Cert no. TT-COC-002303
© 1996 Forest Stewardship Council

A CIP catalogue record for this book is available
from the British Library
ISBN 978-1-908098-17-7

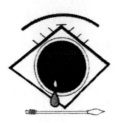

Athina's declaration:

*My legend of resolute courage will trickle down as a
river of gold through the universe until the end of time.
Therein of each generation of females born within my city
of protection called Athens, there will be one who will
know she has been chosen to bear my eyes of beauty, my
resolution and virginity. She alone will carry my spear of
victory until released from my bond - the day her work
is complete. Men will naively succumb but there will be
some Athinian born women who identify and honour the
power of her eyes and stand aside for her.*

For Sylvia

Preface

To know modern Greece and its people, one only has to lift a thin veil to uncover ghosts from its past. The legends of the Gods are in the air they breathe, the soil they plough, the olives they harvest and the dignity etched in their faces – and in the eyes of their women.

Odysseus did land on that island of Ithaca.

The Greece of today is still the Land of the Gods - for they are the soul of modern Greece.

Prologue (1994)

Katie Simpson leaned against the stern rail of the island-ferry *Hellas Athina* as it returned to Piraeus. She continued to wave goodbye, but because of her misty eyes, the figure on the receding quay-side had become just a blur. Over to the right, the early morning sunlight started to glint on the golden cross of the Santa Maria chapel, standing high and proud above the small town that embraced the white cliffs. The distant southern tip of the island moved into view, and suddenly through the haze, the dark scar of the rubbish tip jarred her emotions; she shuddered at its memory and turned away wiping those tears, trying to distract the view by staring at the churning phosphorescent wake stretching its finger back to the island that had such a profound effect on her; and possibly her future ... her future? She was determined to make positive decisions back in London. She knew her controller Janus would try and talk her out of leaving, but she couldn't handle Sarajevo, not now; he'll have to find another *favourite niece*. In any case, the firm was changing for the worse, Janus told her. Somehow her whole being had become an empty shell. She appeared to be strong and yet she felt fragile. Enough was enough, and now it was time to catch up with all those missed years; especially now Athina was releasing her. She turned away from the past few days and looked at the families and the couples, laughing and relaxed after their annual holiday on the idyllic Greek island; the couples with their arms around each other, bronzed and happy, gazing across the sea, looking into a secure future together.

She looked back again to where she knew Andrew would be. She was already missing him; or maybe he had been toying with her emotions? Tomorrow he would also be returning to London, and her future, would he be part of it? She longed to get back and be Katie Simpson yet again and forget that capricious Sarah Athina-Beaumont; away from the crazy and empty charade the firm demanded her to play across those lost years. She sighed and moved over to an empty deck-chair, closing her eyes, trying to relax before the chaos of Piraeus, and not think of the past few days when it went so nearly wrong.

Her arrival (five days earlier)

"WHEN SORROWS COME, THEY COME NOT
SINGLE SPIES, BUT IN BATTALIONS".

The island of Petromos - slowly and surely - appeared like a giant turtle rising up through the early morning mist shrouding the Saronic Island. Dark mauve, with just the hint of orange on the creature's back as the awakening sun rose above the distant horizon. White blobs began to shape into houses and Sarah Athina-Beaumont leaned over the car ferry rail as if to get a closer view of her holiday island, watching the blunt bow shearing through the crystal clear water disturbing the swarms of tiny sardines. Suddenly there were trees and splashes of colour as the flowers took shape, and then came the heavy scents of a Mediterranean island. The blue Byzantine cupola roof of the church with its white painted wall, stood stark against the embracing green foliage of the hills beyond. Her eye caught the golden glint of a cross just catching the early sun on the roof of what appeared to be a small chapel hovering on the edge of a cliff high above the town. The early awakening rays painting long orange fingers across the white walls, catching red roofs of buildings snuggled into the hills; sharply her thoughts were broken as the long, deep drone of the ship's siren echoed around the small inlet bay awakening the sleepy town, bringing a flurry of figures onto the dock side as the ferry's loading ramp started its downward thrust, meeting with perfect timing the concrete pad; the scraping and grinding of iron on concrete with the ferry shuddering to a halt. After the movement came the shouting, followed by ropes thrown down to an eager dockhand; the car and lorry engines starting in anticipation. Soon it was a mad bustle of disorganized chaos with vehicles disembarking, the foot passengers fighting their way against the waiting passengers anxious to climb on board.

Sarah struggled down the ramp with her backpack across her shoulders, her suitcase catching the foot slats as she tried winding her way through the throng. The sun was beginning to burn and already she could feel the warmth coming up from the concrete jetty. It heralded yet another glorious day with the promise of a cooling swim in water that already shimmered, catching her narrowed eyes from the low sun. She walked to the top of the quay and turned, as suddenly there was the deep drone from the ferry saying goodbye until its re-appearance later in the afternoon. She watched as the ferry started reversing with the car ramp only halfway up; the lone dockhand coiling a rope; the chaos over for another few hours. She admired the ferry's technique of turning within such narrow waters, its side-thrusters pounding and then heading back on the hour-long return trip to Piraeus; the backdrop of mauve-coloured islands was most magical.

She approached a young port police officer wearing what seemed to be the obligatory wrap-round Ray-Bans. He was leaning against the ticket office doorway flicking his prayer-beads; seemingly bemused by the twice-daily chaos within his jurisdiction; his light blue uniform and tanned face beneath his flat cap making him seem a most handsome figure. The young woman always considered herself as being a slip of a girl but he was much shorter, and when he saw the young attractive woman approaching with a slip of paper in her hand, he touched his cap and smiled; *the smile of the devil, as her mother would say.* Her large dark glasses set against long blond hair; the unusual coppery vellus-layers glowing within the tight locks intrigued his curiosity and as such he fantasized the colour of those hidden eyes. He glanced at the paper with the name Hotel Mira and frowned as he also noticed a faint pencil scrawl, *Oddessa,* across the top

She followed him as he walked over to a gap in the buildings and pointed to a cream-washed building behind the church. He re-turned to resume his leaning, flicking his prayer beads and watching the young lady as she struggled with her luggage until disappearing behind the church. He glanced at his watch and stared at the few remaining confused people still on the jetty; maybe his expectant visitor will be on the later ferry?

As she walked up the hill, a battered red pickup pulled alongside her. A young woman with dark-rimmed glasses called out, 'are you going to the Mira?'

Sarah nodded, and the woman smiled. 'That's where I'm going. Get in.'

'Wonderful,' gasped a grateful Sarah beginning to feel the strength of the early morning sun. She dropped her luggage onto the flat back of the pickup and climbed into the fish-smelling cab.

They turned into waste ground just before the hotel and stopped alongside a bar called Beachcomber. The woman jumped out and grabbed the suitcase. As she put it on the ground she offered her hand. 'You must be Miss Athina-Beaumont, I've been expecting you. My name is Kelena.'

'Oh please, call me Sarah. Of course, we spoke on the phone yesterday and this is your hotel?'

The woman nodded yes and watched as the English woman paused to admire the modern cream building covered by a mass of delightful and pretty mauve bougainvillea hanging and clinging to the walls with its finger tips; the containers of vivid red pelargonium making a blaze of colour in the strong sun; Sarah thought of her few pots of geraniums struggling in the grey light back home on her London balcony. The front terrace had an ancient struggling gnarled olive tree set in the middle with its generous and welcome dapple shade, surrounded by several straw umbrellas offering their relief to the tables that were already beginning to fill with guests enjoying their breakfast. Sarah looked around to collect her bearings. 'I *was* hoping that port official might have helped me. He didn't seem to have anything else to do.'

Kelena angrily tossed her head and glared in the direction of the port. 'Who ... Panos?' she spat the name out. 'He's never done a day's work in his life.' She then smiled. 'You must be tired and hungry. I'll take you to your room, and then you must eat and drink. Come.' She picked up the suitcase. 'Follow me.'

The young English newcomer lingered on her shaded balcony admiring the vacant expanse that stretched across the mauve horizon speckled with white sails just breaking the vacuum; she will grow to learn the distant horizon as being the edge of the world to the islanders. She thought she could just make out the *Hellas Athina* on its return journey back to Piraeus; the foaming phosphorescence cutting a curious white line in the intense blue sea. She had warmed to Kelena. Sarah thought she was perhaps in her late thirties, tall, her black eyes having an end of season weariness behind her dark rimmed glasses; an attractive woman with the tight, drawn-back dark hair emphasizing her sharp classical Greek profile; her English learnt from the street, clipped and friendly. Suddenly the smell of coffee and bacon made her realise how hungry she was. She hurried down into the rather gloomy interior of the bar, noisy with the obligatory television blaring out some senseless game-show. Kelena appeared with a tray heading to the terrace. She smiled and Sarah followed her to a far table under the olive tree.

She glanced around, her trained instinct to analyse and catalogue fellow travellers; the couples were rather older than her, no doubt enjoying freedom from their offspring probably settled into university. Kelena suggested an English breakfast which sounded wonderful. Just then a short, heavy built man in scruffy clothes walked through and nodded to the clients. His sea-weathered face and narrowed eyes from years in the sun indicated his island breeding. He carried a bucket of fish and followed by a slightly built, chalky-faced young man with a feral look about him. He wore a black baseball cap pulled down low over his forehead who glanced at Sarah with sunken red pupils; his uncomfortable and hostile stare gave Sarah an instant bad feeling; *the hunter?* Kelena ignored them and hurried away to get the breakfast. In the shade, on the far side of the terrace, sat two men; one appeared to have a reserved quiet presence and in his late twenties; he had strong lined features and with a subdued dress code in contrast to the other man; pale, pasty-faced, over-weight example of indulgence, perhaps in his fifties. He was dressed unforgivably in pink baggy shorts with a floral shirt, a tourist straw hat that perched comically on the back of his bald head. He turned and stared at the newcomer through frameless tinted glasses. At that distance Sarah could still make out his expressionless milky eyes; they didn't appear to have any colour and she had the impression a blind had been pulled down behind his transparent pupils. Opening a powder compact she studied her face in the mirror ... oh, she did look tired after that hurried journey from London, her skin demanding sunshine. She pressed the side of the compact and a small digital image appeared in the mirror of the man still watching; she pressed the side again and repeated with the younger man before snapping the lid shut and dropping it in her bag. The rest of the guests appeared to be normal and she tucked into her breakfast; she was hungry!

An elderly couple rose to leave and the lady with a blue rinse and wide red-rimmed glasses smiled and advanced over. 'I'm Geraldine and this is my husband Harold.' Sarah stood and shook hands. Sarah introduced herself and the lady enquired, 'I assume you are on holiday?'

'Well I just grabbed a last minute break from London ... get a bit of sunshine before the summer is over.'

'Sadly we only have a few days left, but the others here are all very pleasant.'

Sarah raised her eyebrows. 'And how about the strange man with the comic hat over there, behind you, the man who keeps staring at me?'

'Ah, yes him, our Mr. Podolski. Apparently he's from the Ukraine.' She grinned and whispered mischievously, 'I call him *mister creepy*, and the other is Danni. At least they keep to themselves.' Her eyes glanced secretly from side to side as she leaned nearer. 'Apparently

5

he's buying a villa up on the hill overlooking the town. Must have deep pockets for that view I guess.' She straightened up. 'Are you going for a swim Sarah, because that's where we're going?'

'Yes, I can't wait.'

Eager to off-load more news she leaned forward again. 'There was a drowning here on the other side of the island last week. It's all rather sad, of course. An English holiday maker; apparently he was on his own. I think it's best to stick to the beach here.'

For one moment it looked as though she was going to sit at Sarah's table but stopped by her husband's obvious cough. She continued, 'Now my dear, if you like walking, there is a most beautiful spot on the road leading out of town. It's a tiny chapel called Santa Maria and it overlooks the bay. It has the most glorious sea views. We've been up there to watch the sun go down.' She turned to her husband who nodded, beginning to look slightly embarrassed. Sarah tried to sit but the woman was in full flow. 'It's right on the edge of the cliff, so do be careful.' She inclined over and smiled benevolently at Sarah. 'Don't want to lose you so soon … do us, my dear.'

Her husband's gaze changed from resignation to serious. 'I think it's quite *dodgy*! The Greeks don't seem to have safety in mind I'm afraid. Kelena told us to be careful as there have been several accidents up there with tourists;' and with that warning to the new-comer, the couple left for the beach. Geraldine commented quietly to her husband, 'what a charming young woman.' Pausing thoughtful for a moment she nodded her head with a knowing look he had seen many times. 'I suspect she has come here to get away.'

He raised an eyebrow. 'Get away?'

'Yes, get away from a broken marriage my dear. She didn't have a ring; timid little thing; wouldn't hurt a fly and what unusual eyes.'

He stared at her. 'Who gave you this information?'

The lady smiled and tapped the side of her nose. 'Woman's intuition my dear … ah, the water looks lovely today!'

Sarah finished her coffee and watched the couple heading for their swim; Harold's cautionary body language, receding hair line and clipped moustache reminiscent of her bank manager back home, his wife Geraldine was definitely committee material. Sarah doubted if anything would pass by without her noticing; she smiled to herself and continued her breakfast. By then the others had all departed, including Geraldine's *mister creepy,* with what she assessed, as his reticent companion, Danni; interesting couple? She wrote her thoughts down in shorthand on her note-pad as Kelena came to the table and started clearing away. 'Would you like another coffee my dear?'

Sarah nodded and Kelena smiled. 'So could I, I'm dying for a drink. I'll fetch some. Would you mind if I sit with you?'

'Of course not, and you can fill me in with all the gossip.' Sarah closed her note-pad and slipped it into her bag.

The scruffy man in the bar seemed to be obstructive, his voice droning, arguing with Kelena as she made the coffee, but soon she came and sat at the table. 'That is my husband Petra,' her tone surprisingly acerbic. 'He hangs around until it's time to go fishing. He mostly works at night ... thank god!'

'And who is the other man?'

'Ion, he's Romanian and helping Petra with his fishing during this season. He suddenly appeared looking for temporary work so my lazy husband took him on, but he's as lazy as Petra. They deserve each other. He sits at the bar and suggests that I ...' Her black eyes blazed, 'I should go and get their breakfast.' She spat out a word. 'Sorry, that is a Greek bad word. You don't speak Greek do you?'

Sarah ignored the question, casually asking her, 'Does this Ion have another name?'

Kelena shrugged. 'Never heard it mentioned. He has no papers for work permission, but Petra always say damn to papers. He's sly and I don't like him. He gives me the shivers.'

'Does he live in the hotel?'

'He sleeps in the wood store behind the hotel. We have space there for staff, but now the season is nearly over it's only him.' She angrily tossed her head. 'I wouldn't have him *here*,' her voice rose, '*in my hotel!*'

Sarah smiled, changing her conversation. 'Are all Greek men lazy, Kelena?'

Kelena wagged her finger. 'Never marry a Greek man Sarah, you'll soon regret it.'

'I promise.' They both laughed.

Sarah watched from the corner of her eye as Kelena's husband Petra ambled past into the burning sun, followed minutes later by the Romanian called Ion, sulking past, his head lowered to the ground with an air of darkness giving her an unpleasant sensation of cold air on her neck. Kelena ignored him, went back into the kitchen and Sarah made a few more notes.

She noticed Kelena appearing behind the bar with a round, domed ceramic container with holes cut in the top. She lifted the lid and Sarah could see a wick which Kelena lit. She replaced the dome and carried it behind a wall at the side of the bar. Intrigued, Sarah walked over and peered around the bar as Kelena made the sign of the cross. She had her own shrine. Sarah also gave the sign of the cross.

Kelena suddenly turned and smiled at her guest. 'May I explain?'

In the gloom of the bar Sarah removed her dark glasses, nodding. 'Oh please.'

Kelena hesitated as she caught the intensity of the English woman's eyes. 'I light this every morning and I say to the Virgin Mary and Jesus, *"I start a new day"*.' She patted her heart, *'"and you both are still here for me"*.' She pointed to three groups of framed pictures. 'The top contains four icons of the Virgin Mary and baby Jesus.' She made another sign of the cross. 'The large silver frame of course, is Mary and Jesus, but that is very special as it has been handed down for generations through my family.' She indicated with her hand to the large picture mounted onto a silver back-ground. 'St Peter. We live well because of the plentiful fish we are blessed with. We must not forget him,' she paused, 'it is very important.' She rearranged some items and continued, 'the land is divided into many islands, so we are surrounded by the sea, and fishing is there for us all. We are very lucky. And for this we must remember and give thanks. We must not forget.' She nodded her head. 'It is very important.' She re-arranged a ceramic incense burner. She lifted and kissed her prayer book. Sarah took the book and kissed it.

Kelena noticed that the young woman was visibly moved. 'Does it also mean a great deal to you, Sarah?'

'Yes. I'm Catholic ... but it's all the same at the end of the day.'

Kelena agreed and nodded. 'Yes, it's all the same. This is *my* church, not that large building they call a church in the town. Prayer is personal, not to go and make a show in front of other people.' She pointed at Mary. 'She doesn't need a building.' Patting her heart and her black eyes shining she looked at Sarah. 'She wants to hear it from here.' She gestured with a nod to her shrine. 'This is my church, here, where I work hard to feed my family.' Her eyes glared but softened as Sarah handed back the book. 'We are but one small island in hundreds.'

'How many islands are there in Greece?'

Kelena shrugged her shoulders and laughed. 'Who knows? Plato once remarked that the Greek people are frogs sitting around a pond.' Kelena now aware her English guest seemed pensive. 'I think you have conflicts in your life that test your beliefs. But you have no choice, am I right?'

Sarah nodded. 'It took a long time to come to terms with what I have to do,' and then as if her mind was of another time, she quietly said, '... but *she* understands and approves.'

Kelena frowned. 'And what do you do?'

Sarah suddenly came back to where she was, looking at the woman, smiling. 'Sorry Kelena, I got carried away. Look, I'm keeping you from your work and I'm dying for a swim ... after London, I can't wait.'

Kelena suddenly hugged the young woman. 'It is so nice to talk to you Sarah. I know in my heart you are a good woman, I can feel it. It will turn out well in the end ... believe me. I will make a special prayer for you when I say goodnight to her.'

'Thank you Kelena. I would like that. In fact, I would like that a great deal.'

The Greek hotel owner watched the young English woman with her dark green Athina eyes heading down to the beach. There was something unsettling that she couldn't understand; she would have to wait and see. She sensed an unfavourable omen. She turned and gave the sign of the cross, making that special prayer for her English guest; not wanting to wait for later that night.

On her way to the beach, Sarah had slipped into the island's only phone booth opposite the Beachcomber bar to make a note of the number, trying to ignore the human smell of sweat and beer. Later, as she relaxed, she became aware of a shadow casting through the straw-thatch of the umbrella and jerked, automatically her hand dropping into her bag. The port police officer Panos stood dripping with his back to the sharp sun and it was at first difficult to see his face. His towel hung round his neck, his dark glasses perched on top of his wet dragged-back hair; she couldn't help thinking he was decidedly overweight.

She put her hand up, shielding her eyes and stared back. 'Well?'

He smiled, taking in her bikini which made her uncomfortable so she pulled the towel further over her legs. He gestured apology by looking away. 'I didn't realise you were my visitor,' he offered, shrugging and wiping his face with the towel, 'I would have carried your luggage to the hotel.'

She tossed her head and grimaced irritably. 'OK if you say so Panos.'

'I was expecting …' he seemed uncomfortable, 'well someone different, but I recall seeing *Oddessa* written on your slip of paper and—'

'I don't want you to be seen talking to me,' she interrupted. She glanced along the beach. 'Go and pester those two girls along there. You might have better luck.'

He glanced along the beach. 'I'll see you tomorrow morning

then.' He nodded and re-adjusted his Ray-Bans to saunter with a fixed smile along to the two unsuspecting teenagers who giggled as he sat down. Sarah watched them for a moment and then sank back into the sand. 'Thank goodness I'm past that age.'

Later that evening before dinner and the expectant rush, Sarah asked Kelena about a cove called Ingissy on the other side of the island. 'A friend in London said it was quiet and with good swimming.'

She nodded. 'Yes, it is very good, but did you hear of the drowning one week past. I would be very careful. Something strange about it, and according to the police it was a simple accident, so be very careful. How are you getting there? It is too far to walk ... in this heat!'

'Is there a scooter I could hire?'

Kelena smiled. 'You can borrow my Grigona, or my Petra.' She giggled at Sarah's expression. 'That's my scooter! I call it Grigona which I think means fast in English. And if it no start, I call it Petra because I kick it in anger. It make me feel better.'

Sarah loved her description and laughed at the image.

This made Kelena laugh again. 'Ah it is so nice to laugh with you. We can have fun Sarah. I knew when we first meet we get on. I won't need Grigona tomorrow. And I'll give you a packed lunch and water.'

Sarah expressed her thanks and Kelena continued. 'It is also a little cove where the island fishing boats are moored. That's where my husband Petra keeps his boat. There is a small island that you can get to over a wooden bridge. It is private and an English man lives there. He is, how you say, a recluse. A writer or painter but we don't see much of him. He has a housekeeper, and her husband is the odd job man. They come into town for shopping but very rarely him. They also have a guard dog so keep away from the island. What time would you like to leave?'

'I need to do some shopping in the town but I would I like to get there after ten.'

'It takes about half an hour, so I'll have it ready for you in time.' Kelena continued her serving and Sarah noticed Geraldine's *mister creepy* staring and standing in the doorway with his companion; she shuddered and turned her head away; what was it about him? The young man left him there and made for an empty table. He checked the setting of the cutlery and pulling out a chair he nodded. The man came over and sat down with his back to her. The young man took the napkin and laid it across the older man's lap and then sat in the opposite chair. She found cruel satisfaction in the man's shiny pink face and with the obvious discomfort as he moved; he wouldn't be sun-bathing the next day. Sarah watched this apparent ceremony with detached amusement as Kelena slipped a map of the island on her table. As she waited for her meal she sipped her beer and studied the area around the cove called Ingissy.

Later that night after all the guests had retired and when the bar suddenly went quiet, she slipped down to the reception and studied the hotel register. She cast her eye over the spare key board behind the desk and hurried back to her bed.

2

'... an impressionist painting of Ingissy'

A slight, cool mist drenched the island, absorbing heat from the early morning sun. The young English woman with the name of *Sarah Athina-Beaumont* on her passport, dressed only in T-shirt and shorts, pulled off the road to stop alongside the chapel of Santa Maria perched on the cliff edge. Yes, Geraldine was right, it did have the most glorious views, and she was determined to spend time there before her stay on the island ended. She continued along the bumpy and dusty road, eventually turning onto a track she had noticed on Kelena's map. This led through the pines and undergrowth to a clearing by the edge of the headland slope that enabled her to look down into the cove and across to the tiny island known as Ingissy without being seen. A green tiled roof raised its head above olive trees and the tall eucalyptus trees that hid the island. She tucked Grigona, or Petra, behind a bush, still amused by Kelena's description of the moped, and sat scanning the area with her binoculars. She looked at her watch ... ten-thirty. The cove was indeed picturesque, beautiful and unspoilt, with an untidy grouping of small fishing boats, gently swinging in the aquamarine sea; their highly coloured red and green painted hulls mirrored in the shimmering water. Framing the shore to the left, a jetty ramp that appeared to hang over the water, and at its side a concrete block hut used by the fishermen; an assortment of lobster pots and nets laid out to dry in the coming sun against the backdrop of pine trees, completed, in her artistic mind, a flawless impressionistic painting making emotional play with her senses.

No apparent movement of life in the tranquil scene; no indication that a man had drowned there just one week earlier. A lizard made her jump as it ran across her open sandals. It turned and stared with bulging eyes. She admired its green body with black stripes across the tummy; a female? For a moment they contemplated each other. She knelt down and asked, 'are you looking for your mate, little one? Are you lonely like me?' She invited her new friend's enquiring eyes, 'join the club.' It turned and disappeared as quickly as it had arrived. She continued to study the island joined to the mainland by a rickety wooden bridge. On the island side of the bridge, stood a tall, rusty Iron Gate, shut firmly tight with a large padlock and chain to deter any curious holidaymakers; the message made clear with *Private* chalked across a drooping sign tied with string to the rusting iron. She spotted the movement of a guard dog by the gate sniffing the air; could it sense her?

Sarah took a swig of water from her bottle and heard a vehicle crunching along the road behind leading down to the beach. An old battered pickup appeared and parked next to the hut. A figure got out and headed for the wooden bridge. The dog barked and a man looked out from behind the gate, chaining the animal to a kennel. He unlocked the padlock, opening the gate that grated against its reluctant hinges to let the visitor in; Sarah nodded in recognition. She waited and scanned to see if any other figures would appear in the cove now that the visitor was in, or if he had been followed; all appeared quiet. She removed her top and shorts, stuffing them into a waterproof backpack. She was already dressed in her bikini. She tied back her hair, adjusted her sunglasses, and glancing at her watch she scrambled down the slope and silently slid into the fresh warm water. Her earlier calculation that in the morning, the sun would be reflecting off the sea and dazzling any watchers on the island proved correct. Suddenly two cars drew up on the jetty-ramp with holiday makers jumping out, lots of shouting and screaming from young kids distracting any watchers from the island; perfect timing! She quietly swam until she found herself around the far point of the island. There was no movement above as she pulled herself into a small inlet and changed into the dry clothing from her back pack. Stuffing the pack into a cleft in the rock she started to climb.

The white-washed villa, with its green pantiles, sat on top of a nap discreetly hidden from the holiday makers enjoying the beach behind. She paused for a moment to take in the mesmeric view of the open sea and the wide terrace that graced the south-facing vista. A large colourful awning offered its shade to a wooden table and chairs; an easel and canvas standing on the side together with a bar billiard table completed the setting. She smelt cigar aroma and could just see the figure of a young man she recognised from London lying nearby in the shade of a huge Eucalyptus tree. He appeared oblivious to the visitor as she quietly walked past him and onto the terrace. Through the open sliding door came the sound of voices and occasional laughter.

As she reached the top step she felt a sharp metallic prod in her back and a voice with a London twang whispered, 'OK darling, this is as far as you go.'

The next moment, the voice was pinned to the ground with his arm twisted behind his back, the gun pressed hard against his skull.

'I'm not your darling,' she spat out. 'Don't ever try to creep up behind me again. I could have taken you out minutes ago as you slept under that tree.' She gave his arm an extra twist and he groaned.

'OK! OK! Sorry!'

The sound of the man hitting the ground and his groaning brought a large figure hurrying out through the sliding door. He was in his sixties, head-shaven, deeply tanned and dressed only in paint-splattered white baggy shorts, his large belly being his dominant feature. His craggy face with sunken eyes was that of a man who had lived mostly on the edge. A large broken nose, reflecting the career of his youth in the ring, hovered over his fleshy mouth of bad teeth. He stared at the sight before him and started to grin. He was quickly followed by two other gawping men.

She stepped back and her assailant pulled himself back onto his feet nursing his bruised arm. Sarah hissed, staring into the young man's surprised face, 'just keep your hands where I can see them. Next time I won't be so gentle.' She handed back his gun. 'I'll talk to you later, don't get lost.'

He glared at her, turned on his heels and headed back to the Eucalyptus tree.

Panos, the island policeman, stepped forward. 'When did you get here? I thought you weren't coming. I didn't see a car. We've been watching the bridge.'

'Well I saw you arrive at ten forty-five to be precise.' She looked at her watch. 'Actually I'm five minutes late. I would have been on time, if I hadn't had to deal with one of your garden lizards.'

The large man towered over her and laughed. 'I like what you did to old Ricki there. Bruised his ego I bet,' his voice deep with a London accent. 'Come on in. I'm Johnnie ... fancy a beer?'

She took in the untidy room, smelling of stale whisky, old magazines, videos and a large television in the corner, the walls covered with amateurish acrylic paintings. Johnnie noticed her looking and hopefully commented, 'they're all mine. Not bad eh? It's the one thing that stops me going mad in this forsaken hole. I sell quite a number in Athens, mainly to the Brits on holiday and signed with a Greek name. Ironic really, can't sell under my own name of course, so I sign them after that Greek painter, *Aristotle*.'

Her eyebrows shot up as she stared at the crab-like scrawl across the bottom. 'Aristotle the painter!' she exclaimed.

He nodded. 'Sure. Reckon I would get more if they knew who really painted them.' He smiled, recalling his past criminal notoriety.

She turned and looked out taking in the stunning view. 'Forsaken hole you call this?'

'You try living here. Can't go out ... can't have me old mates here, so who can I trust? When you've seen that same view over the years, it gets boring; yeah ... as I said ... *boring!*'

The third man left the room, but quickly returned with a glass of cold lager that Sarah gratefully sipped. She stared at them. 'As you could imagine, London is not very happy about losing one of its people. It seems as if the whole operation has been botched. In fact, Janus is fuming. One of us ... shot dead and you say you know nothing ... nothing!' Her voice became edgy. 'He's demanding answers!'

She knew she fell down on interrogation. Her tutor told her she was too brusque and suffered fools gladly, especially when she saw obvious stalling; at that moment she couldn't care less; she was still peeved with that Ricki trying to show her up on the terrace.

Johnnie pulled his baggy shorts up over his belly then raised both hands. 'Don't get me involved with this. Your lot's supposed to be looking after me. Giving me protection! Anyway, since when was he shot? We were told he'd drowned.'

Panos hovered by the patio door. He spoke up, 'We didn't even know someone was coming. He didn't come through the port, and how do you know he was shot?'

'The Greek government wouldn't want it known about a shooting on one of its holiday islands; got to think of tourism. It suited them to leave it as a drowning.' She paused for effect. 'It was a tiny dart shaped bullet and only noticed by a thorough autopsy.'

Panos frowned. 'Tiny?'

She nodded. 'Yes, fired by a pneumatic pistol that's been developed in Romania from an old Czech system by Kolibri. It's almost silent with virtually a non-traceable entry. So it appears we have Romanian involvement.'

Johnnie wiped his sweating brow. 'Yeah, well there's plenty on the island. Pity that bloody wall had to come down; first Russians, and now bloody Romanians. Next it'll be little green men from Mars.' He glanced around waiting for laughter, but they just stared at the woman from London.

Sarah continued. 'He landed by boat during the night on this island, the way I came in. I've seen the boatman's report and he states he left the agent here. His report confirmed no moon and as arranged he waited quarter of a mile off shore, watching to make

17

sure all was OK. He was unsure what to do after the agreed time was up so he returned to Piraeus. First thing next morning, the body was found floating in the sea near here and all hell broke loose back in London. The post-mortem suggested he died about the time he landed, so his killer must have been waiting for him.'

The conversation stalled until broken by a passing fishing boat, its distant, throbbing diesel engine and splashing shoreline waves somehow surreal; unemotionally discussing the death of a man. She studied the three men: Panos dressed in dirty jeans, a white shirt that had known better days and dark with stain. His face pinched with blue stubble showing glistening sweat; he didn't look quite so handsome now. Johnnie sat down, staring into the red tiled floor, red blotches on his neck showing through his tan ... a worried man ... something to hide?

She stared, assessing him. The department had been looking after him for two years now and that was the price they had to pay to nail other gang leaders. It had worked but after two years they wanted him off their hands. Janus's budget was stretched with all the cut backs and he just couldn't afford it. Major Bentley-Snade had instructions from the Prime Minister directly to look for cuts in the Greek department as they had been somewhat quiet the past year. Janus complained it was like taking a fence away, because they had no proof it had actually stopped anybody falling off a cliff.

The man before her appeared edgy; ruthless in London with tentacles stretching up to Scotland. He wasn't to be trusted; used to getting his own way and the unit's psychiatrist warned her, he would now feel as if in a cage. His face showed his resentment with someone else being in the driving seat; a mere slip of a woman interrogating him - *him* - *Johnnie Flynn*. When he walked down the streets of Soho, people would move aside with concern – he mistakenly assumed as respect - his right. Janus said he was getting telepathic vibes from Johnnie. He was correct, she was also getting those vibes and it made her feel uncomfortable; always after the main chance, he couldn't be trusted.

The third man called Henry was in his fifties, short and swarthy with leaden eyes and an ugly scar down one cheek, dressed in torn jeans and a sweat-stained shirt bearing a faded *Gunners* logo across his chest; odd job man for want of a better title. He was Johnnie's right hand man back in London, keeping Johnnie's gang on their toes and devotee to his boss; a dog with his master at his beck and call she thought. She had checked their background files for info at the unit before she caught the first available flight out.

The three studied the slightly-built girl perched on the chair enjoying Johnnie's beer. They knew a female operator was coming from London and somehow were expecting maybe an Amazon woman. But having seen her in action a few moments earlier, they watched, unsure and trying not to be caught within her intense gaze.

She took another sip of her lager and continued. 'OK. Tell me what happened?'

The three started to talk at once. She pointed to Johnnie. 'Let's start with you then, Johnnie.'

He couldn't add to anything because he was sleeping off a heavy night. He and Henry had been playing whist and had seen the dawn in, having downed two bottles of cheap whisky; or *Gold Watch* as he called it. Henry's wife Rose had been busy preparing breakfast when the bodyguard Ricki came in to answer the phone about eight o'clock; Ricki being the only person allowed to take a call.

Panos interrupted. 'I'll get Ricki in.'

She shook her head, and commented sarcastically, 'No. I'll go and wake him up.'

She returned to the garden glad to get away from the over-bearing presence of Johnnie, catching a waft of cigar smoke and the soft sound of a harmonica led her to the Eucalyptus tree. The young agent Ricki was sitting on a chair gazing out to sea, absorbed in his playing. He jumped up as he became aware of her presence. He put the cigarillo in his lips, dropping the organ into his shirt top pocket.

Before she spoke, she pushed the glasses onto her hair

preferring to look at him direct. 'You realise you'll be returning back to the grime and grey of London,' she snapped. She swept her eyes across the stunning backdrop. 'You won't have this view from your backyard.'

Because of her anger and his sore arm, he was trying not to show his fascination with those piercing dark-green eyes. He was aware of her reputation but didn't think they would be sending her. He held his arm which was throbbing.

'I could have been anyone, and you're supposed to be on duty. You knew I was due at eleven, yet you were dozing. Sleeping off a heavy night I suppose.'

He protested. 'I wasn't ... dozing ma'am!'

'What's the difference?'

'We were expecting you to come over the bridge. I was waiting for a shout from Panos.'

She stiffened. 'Call yourself a bodyguard. You don't assume anything. I swam across because I wanted to see how good the security was. I could have been an intruder out to cause trouble. So I would have dealt with you before going into the house. I knew you were here because of the smell from your cigar.' She leaned forward, snatched it from his mouth and threw it over the parapet wall. 'And on your watch one of our field agents died ... shot ... right under your nose!'

He went to protest, but left his mouth open realising it wouldn't help. He was aware the others in the villa would have heard and the so called dream posting was becoming tenuous.

Her voice rose. 'I hear there's a posting in Russia that's just come in. Guess who's going to get that job?' She sat on the wall. 'Now tell me, where were you when that phone call came in?'

'In bed ... and yes before you say it, I did have a heavy night.' He pulled a face. 'There's not much else to do here and ...' he nodded back to the house. 'Johnnie keeps passing the whisky round.'

'And the phone call?'

'It was Panos. He said fishermen had found a body off-shore when they returned from their night's fishing. Police were coming over from the neighbouring island and he would wait for them; a warning just in case any reporters start nosing around. I went down to the landing area and the body had been taken into the fishermen's building. Luckily, it was too early for holiday makers. I managed to look at the body before Panos and the two policemen arrived. I assumed it was a straight case of a holiday drowning. Panos later told me one of the policemen had commented, that from his experience, he didn't think the man had drowned. I overheard you say the autopsy discovered he had been shot. That I can't understand, there was no sign of a bullet entry. Then Janus rang to say he was one of our agents. I bet that had him jumping around back at HQ!' He frowned. 'I understand it still stands as a drowning?'

Sarah nodded. 'Yes. The Greek government tried to play it down, but you can't keep that quiet, not on a holiday island like this. The uranium bullet is tiny, extra long and dart shape adding to its velocity, and so designed at the rear that the entry hole closes up on itself. The body was waterlogged making the entry at first impossible to spot, so it has to be a trained assassin. Only that type of person would have access to that gun as there can't be many around. London has only just heard about them and the killer would know exactly where to place the shot so a normal autopsy couldn't find it.'

'So what was he doing? Panos said he wasn't staying on Petromos.'

'He came to give your Johnnie a message from London. Why he had to come from a boat and not come as a tourist? Janus thinks he was playing at being James Bond. But what does concern us, has it compromised Johnnie's bolt hole? He's the one that should be worried. Having just met him I couldn't care less. I need to know where he was shot, because our info is, he landed on this little island and died about the same time. So was someone waiting for him? Knew he was coming; or he intruded on something? I want Johnnie's island searched, where did he land exactly? Maybe there's something to help us. Apparently the dart is fired from a centre-fire cartridge. Hedge Farm suggests we look for this cartridge;

and they are desperate to actually get their hands on the gun. The boatman said he couldn't be sure where he landed because it was too dark, but it's possibly the area where I landed. Personally I'm getting bad vibes from Johnnie. He knows more than he's letting on. I think he's up to something. A leopard like him never changes its spots.'

She felt in her pocket and pulled out a small sealed plastic bag. 'Talking of Hedge Farm, take this bug. They want us to give a field test and try out a new satellite communication gadget I've got back in the hotel.'

He studied the bag. 'What am I supposed to do with it then?'

'Press it onto any window glass and it's supposed to pick up the vibrations from voices. Has a transmission range of about half a mile but they think it could be more; Janus seems excited by it. Before I return home I have to record and send a message via the satellite straight back to London; keep the boffins happy.'

'Are we supposed to get excited and when will we have time?'

She was irritated. 'We'll have to make time. It's only an experiment. Keep them happy.'

He dropped it into his shirt pocket. 'How did you get here? I didn't see a boat.'

'I swam of course.'

He looked at her dry clothes and she replied, 'Just work it out. Go and start searching ... thoroughly ... and don't handle anything either.'

He nodded. 'Yes ma'am.' She shrugged her shoulders and turned away. Considering this, their first ever meeting had been fraught, he surprised himself by enjoying her closeness but finding those eyes disturbing. He sensed an awareness of pleasure with the sun catching the coppery sheen within her hair as she walked across the garden. He sighed and leaned over the parapet for his cigarillo, still smouldering and caught on a branch of cotton-wood.

The English woman swam slowly back, savouring the pleasure of the warm crystal-clear water, disturbing shoals of tiny anchovies that had scattered from the thrashing limbs on the small beach to her right. Unnoticed by the holidaymakers she pulled herself out and scrambled back to the top of the slope she had left earlier. She turned and noticed a glint as the midday sun caught the binoculars she guessed would be his trained on her from the island. She only knew him vaguely from the London unit. Their paths had never crossed before and now in a strange way she felt sorry they had got off on the wrong foot. She tried telling herself he needed reminding, out here she was senior to him; or maybe she had found his presence disturbing and she was going to keep him an arm's length away; like all the others. She carefully studied the area around her moped; no sign of disturbance. She sat down and suddenly felt tired, gratefully opening the lunch Kelena had prepared as the shouting and screams from the children rose up to greet her. Maybe she had been over the top with him … a supposed dream posting and stuck with Johnnie despite the view. He had been there with Johnnie for two months instead of the usual one. Janus had surprised her by leaving him there. It wasn't the 'firms' policy to leave agents too long with people like Johnnie who had a history of corrupting all those he came in contact with. She had a gut feeling Janus was going to pull the rug from under his little hide-away very soon.

Changing back into her shorts and T-shirt, she removed a small Beretta from her pack. She fitted the silencer, twisted it tight and loaded one of the clips. Taking a swig from the plastic water bottle, she placed it on an embankment of gravel, then walking back about twenty paces she suddenly swung round, crouched and took aim; the puff of dust was two inches to the right. She studied the pistol and the bottle, again crouched, aimed and fired. This time the neck shattered; her eye and aim still good. She enjoyed the moment as opportunities away from the firing range were rare and she felt satisfaction as she retrieved the bottle and took another swig.

'... room eleven the panic suite'

The steady, rhythmic chopping of vegetables in the kitchen, made Sarah call out, 'Kelena is that you?'

'Hi, yes it's me alright.' Kelena looked around the doorway and smiled, her round face behind the large dark-framed glasses reminding Sarah of Nana Mouskouri. 'Ah Sarah, how did you enjoy your day?'

'It was lovely and I had lots of swims. What a pretty place. Thank you so much for the loan of Grigona, I didn't have to kick it.' They both laughed. 'And boy, did your lunch taste good! Greatly appreciated! I'm afraid I broke the plastic bottle.'

She laughed. 'No problem, we don't have a shortage of plastic bottles here for sure. Would a certain English lady like *a nice cup of tea?*'

'Sounds heaven,' exclaimed a grateful Sarah.

'Oh Sarah, I had a call from your uncle.' She peered at a scrap of paper. 'Uncle Alec? He said if you have the time, he is in Athens tomorrow on business and would love to see you in the morning ... at a bar called Oddessa ... easy to find. I know Oddessa, it's by the Acropolis and I'll give you directions.'

Kelena made Sarah a pot of tea which she carried out and sat under a straw umbrella, hiding away from the sun with an intensity that she found uncomfortable; the summer in London had been noticeable by its lack of sunshine. She sipped her tea and made a few notes. Her departure from London had been swift. The alarm bells had started to ring early that particular morning, and she hadn't even had time to remove her coat before she was told to report to *Room Eleven* on the top floor, known as the Panic Suite; only used when there was a flap on. Janus told her about the dead agent and his mission; Sarah didn't even know he was out of the country. Her controller had the appearance of a jovial uncle and known simply as Janus. There's no doubt he had a favourite *niece* in the girl sitting before him. He picked her out from several applicants that wanted to join the island unit set up after the fall of the Berlin Wall.

She was born in Greece to diplomatic parents and spent her first twelve years in Athens, and as such, fluent in the language. The physical training had shown her to be competitive, particularly coming top on the shooting range; as such, her reputation for resolve and utter dedication to her work went before her. Her real name was Katie Simpson, but out in the field her cover became Sarah Athina-Beaumont; the service obsessed in keeping its agent identities secret.

When she joined the Field Unit seven years earlier straight from university, she had to choose her new identity. Her choice was easy, she decided to use her grand mamma's christian name of Athina and combine it with her maiden name of Beaumont; how tickled pink grand mamma would have been. She had also inherited the unusual slate-green eyes of the females in her family; she would break many a heart she was told. Her slight appearance belied her implausible career, with friends and family assuming her to have a gentle, secretarial position in the Greek section of the Business Attaché's office in Whitehall; the odd travel to Greece as a perk, but surely stuck all day in front of a keyboard. Her ex-diplomatic father wasn't fooled but never said a word to her mother; didn't stop him worrying though.

It seemed a lifetime ago when her studies at New College, Oxford were ending after three years of Greek classics, her thoughts concentrating on her coming dissertation; those thoughts went out the window on a bright summer morning when she was intrigued by a mysterious note slipped under her door containing

25

a telephone number. A woman answered inviting her to lunch.

As they sat down, the curious Katie immediately asked, 'why just the telephone number; supposing I hadn't bothered to ring?'

The woman smiled. 'That was your first test. Nine out of ten would have torn it up or put it on one side to do later. We're not interested in that person. But you were instant. Curious, as you are now. We're interested in an inquisitive mind; instant reaction. We know all about your Greek background, your fluency and as your studies are coming to an end, we thought you might like a few weeks break in the country on a farm.'

The fascinated Katie asked, 'We?'

'Like-minded people.' She grinned at the young girl, taking in the excitement in her unusual eyes. 'Don't tell me you're not curious?'

Katie was and replied, 'Yes I'm curious, but also curious about you. You are either some obscure cult or even some government intelligence department.'

The woman nodded and held up a security badge. 'I wouldn't normally show this to you on our first meeting, but I've done my homework and feel confident you will accept.'

She was right of course and Katie then realised that this was the moment her grand mamma had predicted when she was a young girl, on an early morning at the entrance of Athina's Temple.

She couldn't wait to take up the offer. The woman took out a sheet of paper. 'Katie this isn't actually a legal document, it's simply a reminder of your obligations to your country.'

She signed the *Official Secrets* then and there; this was her recruitment to the shadowy world of MI6 – and her new identity – Sarah Athina-Beaumont.

Before she knew what was happening she was at Hedge Farm, working hard on the firing range and learning to pin assailants to the ground as Ricki found to his discomfort. As part of her induction Sarah had to go through the usual medical routine and the ophthalmologist expressing fascination with her eyes and suggesting an involvement with his students; this was immediately jumped on by the Unit, wanting to protect their agents. She soon found herself attached to the newly formed specialised unit dealing exclusively with the Greek islands following in the wake of the Soviet Union break up. And that is when she first came across Janus.

So here she found herself … *Room Eleven*, with yet another overnight flap. She sat opposite Janus - her controller. On his left sat the political director Major Bentley-Snade, the link to the PM. She always thought this exceptionally tall, frail figure of a man was better suited as a character from a Dickens's story. After all the years of looking down at people he stooped slightly, even when seated. He stared at her with his cold uninteresting eyes, not speaking just making notes; she always found his presence unnerving and wished he would just disappear. It was obvious what Janus thought of him from her controller's body language, and from past comments he didn't trust him either. Suddenly the major looked at his fob watch, carefully slipped the pad into his briefcase and without saying a word, rose, and quietly left the room, Janus smiled at her. 'He's done his official politicking so he leaves not wanting to hear my real instructions so the PM can honestly say he has no knowledge should things go wrong; crazy world.'

A crazy world she could never get to grips with, preferring to be away from her desk, out in the field as Sarah Athina-Beaumont.

She had been watched by Geraldine, who was sitting on her balcony; knitting and listening to husband Harold's snoring from the bedroom enjoying his siesta. She thought the young girl looked tired and had a somewhat demure appearance. She seemed to be writing. *A letter, probably to her husband, or soon to be, ex-husband. Oh what tales we weave. Hope she doesn't get pestered by that Romeo, the port police officer. That's the last thing she needs.* She had observed him trying to chat Sarah up on the beach, but had obviously been given cold shift as he abruptly left to pester two other girls nearby. *Good for her!* This morning she had watched Sarah ride off on Kelena's moped to another part of the island, *obviously to keep away from the island's Romeo*. She tried to concentrate on her knitting, but continued to watch and groaned when Panos walked up the steps onto the terrace. He paused by the young lady's table and touched his cap. 'Oh why can't he leave the young girl alone,' she grumbled out loud to her sleeping husband. Panos bent down and picked up something Sarah must have dropped, put it back on the table, touched his cap and went into the bar.

Sarah opened the envelope Panos had pretended to pick up and looked inside. It contained one cartridge that would have held the tiny uranium dart she had seen recovered from the autopsy in London, together with Ricki's hand written note –

I found this on the same stretch of rocks you swam from. Looks like the 4mm as discussed??? Only handled by tweezers ... I promise.

She smiled at his assurance; perhaps she had been too hard on him. *I think I would get bored stuck on that small island with only Johnnie and his side-kick for company despite the glorious setting.* Her eyes shone; *perhaps I won't recommend him for Russia, not that there ever was a Russian posting coming up.*

She went into the bar and found Panos deep in conversation with Petra. She noticed the Romanian lurking quietly in a darken corner, staring at her with unblinking eyes from beneath his baseball cap; again that uncomfortable chill. Panos turned and looked at the English woman. He smiled. 'Hello, may I buy you a drink?'

'No thank you. I was wondering what time the early ferry left for Piraeus tomorrow?'

Panos raised both hands in despair. 'Please, you are not leaving us so soon. You have brightened up our little island by coming here.'

'I will be back in the afternoon. Meeting a friend in Athens on a business trip,' she emphasised.

He grinned. 'I see, a man friend?' He winked at Petra. 'It leaves at nine. You should be in Piraeus just after ten.'

Geraldine continued watching as Sarah returned to her table and sipped her tea. 'Hope she hasn't arranged to meet him,' she called out to her husband.

'Pardon?' he replied, and continued his siesta.

4

' … *Athens and Uncle Alec*'

Piraeus: the usual bustling confusion of activity that Sarah had known as a young girl, but now one big difference; many illegal immigrants from Africa. They were plying for trade on the road leading across to the Stathmos rail station directly opposite the tall iron gates of the dock entrance. Their wares of pirated CDs and DVDs, colourful beads, clockwork toys, cheap imitation Rolex watches all making her passage difficult; the various exotic clicking-tongues ringing in her ears and the many black faces with their waving arms making her progress confused. She felt vulnerable and clutched her bag tightly under her arm. The vinegary sweat from the crowd clung in the heat of the mid-morning sun and mingled with the hanging dust, making her glad to get into the station where the air seemed fresh and strangely clean. She caught the metro to the Acropolis and headed straight to the peace of Oddessa bar, drinking down a glass of chilled water before ordering an Americano coffee.

She rose early that morning to catch the ferry, watching fascinated again with the ramp slowly descending and hitting the concrete jetty with the usual perfect timing. Panos came over and stood by her side, fingering his prayer beads, admiring the way she was dressed in a cream blouse, red choker and tailored cream skirt and open flat shoes; her straw hat with a wide brim shading her eyes from the low sun. Her large sunglasses completed the look of a holiday maker. She turned to him. 'Who actually found the body and reported it? You never told me.'

'Petra. He rang me. But it was actually found by Ion.'

She glared at him. 'Ion! You didn't say.'

'You didn't ask.'

'Don't play games with me. How did he find it? Was he on his own? I thought you said it was discovered by returning fishermen. Petra must have been with him?'

She noticed a slight flush around his neck. 'No. It appears Petra went out on his own because Ion didn't turn up the evening before. He said he'd overslept; drunk more like it, as this often happens. So Petra couldn't wait because the timing for the fish is crucial for a good catch.'

'If Ion wasn't there, how come he discovered the body?'

'He was waiting on the quay early the next morning to help unload the catch.'

Sarah fumed. 'What do you mean by early?'

He pulled a face. 'They normally land their catch by six.'

She was angry. 'So he couldn't have been drunk the night before. He must have been hanging around there during the night when our agent landed. He must know what happened ... or he's our killer. Maybe our agent stumbled onto something or he was mistaken for the opposition here; our friends the Russian mafia.' She kept her voice low, 'if you concentrated on your work instead of playing the local Romeo. You get paid to be our eyes and ears. God, you all make me so mad! And when did this Ion appear on the scene?'

'We don't know anything about him. He turned up one day looking for work and Petra took him on for the summer season. I can't remember him coming off the ferry; especially someone as questionable as him.'

She pulled a face. 'Very convenient I would say. You're supposed to let us check up on people like him. Maybe you would like a trip to Russia,' she snapped striding to get on the ferry.

Now sitting in the shady corner of the Oddessa bar, away from the sun, she pushed that encounter out of her mind and looked up at the high wall rising powerfully above her where the Acropolis and her Parthenon perched, proudly displaying its influence and magnificence even after thousands of years. The marble columns defying all that the weather and mankind could throw at it. Man interfering and restoring over the past two hundred years yet having to return and re-do again and again; it was trying to send a message - *just leave me alone. I know just how you must feel, she thought.* She took in the towering cranes; the permanent restoration site. She recalled, as a young girl, climbing the hill with her brother and playing amongst the huge piles of fallen marble, now ringed with World Heritage 'Keep Out' fencing. She felt a wave of sadness. World Heritage paths and World Heritage wooden huts to collect your money, all scrubbed clean, sanitised and becoming just another Disneyland to gawp at. Take the snapshot and move on to Venice or wherever the tour guide took you; like a parcel moved from post to post; just another place to tick off the list; no time to absorb the drama or its history. From an early age Sarah had been aware of an affinity with the crumbling edifice, always drawn to the Parthenon in her young wonderland mind as Athina, reliving the history and seemingly unable to escape the powerful presence of the Goddess. She felt a wave of emotion, recalling her grand mamma taking her to the Parthenon to watch the sun rise, waiting for the exact moment as the sun-ball lifted off the horizon. Together they placed a small olive-tree branch against the Temple entrance. Her grand mamma took her hand and said, 'now Athina will always watch over you ... she will never abandon you Katie. One day, you will understand my words when I tell you that you've been chosen a certain beginning, from which all will follow'... *dear grand mamma, I do understand.*

The proprietor stood watching from the doorway and eventually came over. 'Sarah?' he asked, interrupting her memories.

'Yes?'

He smiled. 'I have a message from your Uncle Alec. He asks if you could meet him at the Chapel of Agios Georgios on Lykavittos

Hill at about twelve-noon. The air is clear today so I think the view will be wonderful.'

Sarah glanced at her watch and reached for her purse. 'Oh thank you ... I still have plenty of time, perhaps I could pay for my coffee now, as I want to do some shopping first.'

'All taken care of, the firm is paying.' He started to move away. 'Any problems ... you have my number?'

'Yes I do. Thank you.'

He left her and welcomed more tourists to the Oddessa.

The young English woman walked into the Plaka district, along the Adrianou to her favourite shop, Byzantino. As she was about to enter, something caught her eye in the window of the art gallery next door. There on an easel sited prominently in the front of the display, was a familiar looking acrylic painting. She shook her head in disbelief at Johnnie's scrawled *Aristotle* in the bottom corner.

Once in the shop she quickly found what she wanted; a small Byzantine gold cross pendant necklace with a small cabochon ruby at each far point, and the centre piece a slate-green cabochon stone set as the eye of *Athina the Goddess*. The young female assistant hung it around Sarah's neck and in the mirror she admired the central stone catching exactly the slate-green colour of her own eyes. She nodded; it was perfect and exactly what she wanted.

The taxi dropped her at the top of Ploutarchou Street. She looked down the slope with its hundreds of steps she had declined to climb that morning. She thought back to when she was a young girl; she would race her brother and her friend Phillip up those seemingly thousands of steps, and always beat them. She shook her head, couldn't do it now especially in this heat. She sat and waited for the funicular cable car to carry her up the interior tunnel to the highest point overlooking Athens.

Mounting the last few steps she walked onto the sudden open terrace of the Chapel of Agios Georgios, the vast stillness of the panoramic expanse toying with her senses; nine hundred feet above the city, recalling her university gliding with that last moment sensation of sudden silence before she pushed its nose down to make its final hissing descent. She walked to the far wall and looked down on that breath-taking glimpse of the Acropolis where she had been sitting one hour earlier; she felt the Parthenon clearly beckoning, drawing her; calling her? She shaded her eyes and looked across to the distant shiny sea of the Saronic Gulf and thought she could just pick out the island of Petromos as a dark mauve blob, just one hour ferry ride away.

Surprisingly the lack of people at that hour went through her mind, too hot up there, with just a couple of tourists and one cheap trinket vendor leaning against the wall. He wore a battered Mexican straw sombrero, its rim shading his heavily unshaven jowls. He appeared lost in thought, the pungent sweet aroma of his Karelia cigarette drifting across to her in the hot still air; she pulled away. The sun burning as heavy as this rock Athina threw down at Hercules; no wolves roamed the hills any more having descended down into the cities of the world. There was no sign of Uncle Alec so she entered the silent coolness of the Chapel and removed her sunglasses. She waited to absorb the darkness before pausing at the Altar making the sign of the cross, recalling the times she would attend the ceremonies of her childhood Greek friends and be an on-looker at the rites of the Greek Orthodox Church. Her parents were strict Catholics but her father encouraged his children to be interested and learn of the shortcoming, and the strength of other religions. It was the foibles of the human character she had learnt from those early days that stood her head and shoulders above her fellow applicants to the Greek unit; *"gossip is information: knowledge is power"* according to Hedge Farm. The others were certainly more worldly qualified academically, but Janus had quickly become aware of her shrewd understanding with the ways of the human instinct and marked her down for the future. She glanced at her watch ... *bit early ... Uncle Alec is always punctual.* Replacing her sunglasses she walked outside to look at the table of trinkets laid out by the only vendor bothered to be there. She picked up a colourful bracelet and slipped it on her wrist. The vendor threw his cigarette butt over the wall and moved in for a sale by suggesting various pieces. A quiet voice at her shoulder murmured, 'suits you my dear ... may I buy it for you?'

Sarah turned and looked into the steel-blue rascally eyes of Janus.

'Oh, uncle! How lovely to see you.'

He doffed his Panama and kissed her on the cheek. He took one pace back and admired her. 'Your holiday is doing wonders. I love the hat Sarah, it suits you.' She removed her sunglasses making him catch her eyes and he couldn't help grinning as he passed money to the vendor; he was wise to her ways of softening him up with those eyes; but he was also aware that in her naivety she had no concept her eyes were her fortune.

'Thank you, uncle.'

She took in her controller who ruled with a rod of iron back in London, dressed in a cream linen suit and sporting his Zingari striped tie. She felt the motto suited him, *"out of darkness, through fire, into light"* ... yes, he did look the perfect uncle.

He looked at his watch. 'Time for lunch I think my dear.'

She always found the panoramic view from the restaurant over-looking Athens awe inspiring and today was no exception; the Oddessa barman was right. She could sense her companion's gaze across the table so she looked at him with her disarming smile. It always felt uneasy acting out this 'uncle and favourite niece' game; he was after all her boss. He listened attentively to her report on the past few days. She fingered the bracelet; he'd never done that before!

He roared with laughter with the description of her first meeting with Ricki. She handed over the envelope containing the small cartridge case, the waiter taking their order and retreating.

Uncle Alec adjusted his half-moon reading glasses to look inside and read the note.

Oh dear...the note ... she had meant to scrap it.

He smiled and murmured, 'sounds as if you were a little rough on him.' He carefully tucked it in his jacket pocket. 'Yes that tiny dart-like bullet that killed our friend is definitely Romanian. It takes a highly trained assassin to use that gun. It's very difficult to find a point of entry if used in expert hands. The Greek forensic didn't spot it, and in any case, they preferred a drowning verdict. We couldn't believe it was simply a case of drowning. The authorities wanted rid of the body because of the bad publicity, and so it was quickly brought back to London giving our forensic a good look. It would be a bonus if you could lay your hands on that gun, Katie.'

She took out her powder compact and slid open a small tray. She took out a tiny film cartridge together with a list of names. 'Could you run these through the computer? These are the people staying in the hotel.' She pointed at the name Ion. 'I'm particularly interested in this Romanian character ... and these two.' She pointed at Podolski. 'Podolski is rather creepy and from the Ukraine, his companion is called Danni. He's also Romanian and interesting.'

'What do you mean by interesting?'

'Difficult to say but I get a feeling he's not what he would like you to think he is; just a feeling that's all. Podolski apparently is building a place up on the hill overlooking the town. It seems as though he's making it permanent. Wonder what the Russians on the island make of him?'

He slipped the cartridge into his pocket nodding. 'We think our friend was a mistaken victim. He made the decision to go straight to the small island thinking it better than going through the port; less noticeable; ironic in the circumstances.'

'What actually is happening with this ... Johnnie?'

He raised his eyebrows with a slight hint of a smile. 'Would you trust him?'

She pulled a face. 'No way! He's bored and it's tempting for him to slip back into his old habits. No opportunities stuck on that island.'

'Well it was his choice! It was either grassing on his mates and getting protection, or a spell of several years at her Majesty's pleasure. He chose the first option which meant we got lumbered with him. I heard he's getting restless, stuck there with just his paintings. I did hear they're pretty good. Did you see any?'

She laughed. 'They're all over the walls. You can't get away from them. Apparently the British tourists in Athens seem to like them. No accounting for taste.' She stared at him with a smile. 'He signs them Aristotle would you believe.'

He took in her comment and chuckled. The waiter hovered nearby and then turned to a party of new customers; the restaurant beginning to get busy. Uncle Alec waited until he was out of ear-shot and lowered his voice. 'Interpol is concerned with the influx of the Romanian Mafia moving into the islands ... his type of company I'm afraid; old habits and all that. It's bad enough with the Russians already on that island. Soon there'll be trouble and he'll have to take sides. 'Upstairs' feel it's time he moved on. Get him away. That's why our friend was going to talk to him, to warn his protection was coming to an end unless he did as he was told; don't be a naughty boy was the message, and to lean on him. Remind him there are still a lot of old acquaintances in London that'll like to get their hands on him.'

Another waiter came with their drinks and moved away.

'He thinks Ricki is there solely for his protection, but it's also really to stop any unsavoury characters getting to him. Talking of Ricki, do you feel he's OK there?' He chuckled again. 'I guess he's unsure about you?'

'I'm surprised he hasn't been given a break, he's been there for two months now. I couldn't stand being cooped up with that Johnnie whatever the view. OK, at the time he made me angry with his laid-back attitude, but it's his first assignment and I think a lesson has been learnt ... hence the comment on the note.'

'I left him there because big changes are on the way but you might need him, so for the moment we'll leave things as they are. I'll let you know as soon as I'm aware of what's happening, which leads me on to my next concern ... the Balkans.'

She frowned. 'The Balkans?'

'As you know, it's tearing itself apart and we're worried now it's getting out of hand. We've had enough problems stemming from there and history has a habit of repeating itself.'

'How does this affect us ... the Greek department?'

'The whole of the European unit is stretched and upstairs want to pinch personnel from us. I have no choice.'

'What are you saying?'

'To put it bluntly, they want to send you to Sarajevo.'

She put her drink down and stared. 'Me? But Sarajevo is under siege?'

He nodded. 'Slight difficulties with the Serbs and the ring of land mines thrown around the city of course but there are ways, right under NATO's nose would you believe; in fact about ten feet under.' He didn't add any more info. 'Their communication is only by dodgy radio and they can't give too much away with the Serbs listening in.' He leaned forward. 'What we need is someone in there to assess the situation from our point of view; real intelligence we can rely on. It's so tricky because the Russians only need an excuse to openly help the Serbs as they're sore, having lost their route to the warm waters of the Med when the Soviet Union collapsed.'

'I thought the Serbs were the bad guys?'

He looked at his watch. 'That doesn't bother Russia, and where is our lunch?' he asked looking around for the waiter. 'We're criticised by the Bosnians for not helping them with arms, but the West is mindful of how the Russians would react; it could be throwing petrol on an ember. Luckily for the Bosnians ... and us, Iran is smuggling weapons in to help their Islamic brothers and this enables us to stand on the touch line and keep an arm's length away; pardon the pun. So when the crisis is over, the question we're thinking is, what happens to all these weapons coming into Bosnia? Where are they going to disappear to? We're trying to be one step ahead of the terrorists before they get their hands on them and we know the IRA is not without connections there. Sorry to be a bore Katie, but here I quote, *"local gossip is information: knowledge is power."*'

Sarah tried not to smile but pulled a face and ran her fingers along the white linen table cloth. She was already having second thoughts about her job and this was yet another complication. He watched the woman and knew what he was asking. As his director had forcefully stated, 'these are desperate times Janus. The whole of mid-Europe could go up.'

'Look Katie I'm only saying this to let you know what has happened in the short time you've been away. But first we must get this Johnnie chap out of our hair, once and for all.'

They sat quietly, watching as the waiter rearranged their cutlery. He disappeared back into a noisy kitchen; the door swinging back and forwards with a clunking note. Uncle Alec coughed and changed the subject. 'And what's your opinion on, this … Panos? Laughingly called, "our man on the island."'

'He thinks he's a lady killer. Good front I suppose, but considered a lazy character. He needs me to shake him up.' At this, Uncle Alec grinned as she continued, 'I warned him this morning I would be dealing with him on my return because he didn't come clean with who discovered the body. He didn't seem to think it was important. I think he's been allowed too much leeway. Being our eyes and ears to see who comes to the island he probably thought it was money for old rope.' Her eyes glared. 'Not anymore!'

Uncle Alec smiled and raised one eyebrow, reading her anger like a book. 'Why, did he try it on with you before he knew who you were?'

'I think he had me in his sights. He soon got the message.'

He tried to hide his smile, put his hand in his jacket pocket and handed over two small 9v batteries. 'I think you'll like this little gadget, it's Hedge Farm's latest toy and they want it tested … I get the impression they think we're only around to try out their precious gadgets. Give one to Ricki. Should you need to ring me, or Ricki, place this by the phone and press the + terminal … it scrambles the call which ties up with my end. Press the - terminal when you finish. You can also use it in a call box.'

She put it in her bag and smiled at him. 'Clever.'

He sighed and muttered, 'I can't keep up with all this technology, it's alright for you youngsters. I also understand that soon they'll be issuing us with special phones about the size of a pack of cards linked up to a military satellite they've just launched. Just think of that! Be great on these islands with no mobile connections.' He paused, pensive. 'In fact it's all changing back home. Bureaucracy is now moving in, technology is taking over and everything is down to paperwork and accountants. I think we've had the good times Katie; it won't be the same anymore. Sarajevo is probably the last time for you to be an old fashioned freelance operative.'

Clenching a fist, her eyes showing fire, she leaned forward, angrily whispering, 'but that's been the best way to glean intelligence going back to the ancient Greeks, despite all these fancy new gadgets.'

He loved those eyes when she was fired up. He nodded. 'Well, you put up a good defence and then I'll take you to the next monthly meeting.' He shrugged his shoulders. 'I've exhausted my arguments.'

The kitchen door clunked open and the waiter emerged at last to serve their lunch.

Uncle Alec studied his niece as she realised how hungry she was. He didn't have any real nieces, or indeed nephews, so enjoyed the occasional uncle meeting with her. His gesture of buying the bracelet was, of course, part of the act, but he found great warmth in the gesture even though it was cheap. He would have liked to have spent more on her, but oh dear, think of the jealousy back in the office; yes, he admitted to himself, he would have loved to have been her real uncle. He then thought of what he was asking her to do, and why the hesitancy? Normally she would have been fired up.

She became aware of his gaze.

He abruptly looked at her wrist. 'Sorry Katie, but I was admiring the bracelet. It looks very nice on you. But don't tell others how much it cost. It looks quite expensive; always let people assume what appears to be the obvious. The less you say the more they will assume. Oh dear, I think I'm giving one of my lectures. Sorry!'

She smiled, and blushed slightly at his obvious warmth. She fingered the bracelet. 'It's lovely uncle ... but then, I'm an expensive girl.'

'… there are daggers in men's smiles'

Panos touched his cap and looked anxiously at her face.

She felt in a good mood after her trip to Athens and she smiled. 'Good evening Panos.'

'Did you have a good day in the big city, miss?'

'Very good, thank you. Managed to catch up with my uncle and he treated me to lunch. Wanted to know how my holiday was going and my assessment of the island.'

He looked anxious again.

She wiped her brow with the back of her hand; the atmosphere had become humid and she looked out to sea, with the gathering white horses. 'I think we might be building up for a storm later, I can sense it.'

'Yes, but not for a couple of days I think.'

'Where can I get hold of you … off duty? Where do you live?'

His eyes lit up.

'Don't get any ideas Panos. Things could happen soon and you might be needed.'

He pointed to the side of the church. 'There. That small Spiti. It comes with the job. If I'm not there, you can usually find me at the bar opposite your hotel, the Beachcomber.'

Is that where that sidekick of Petra hangs out during the day?'

'Side-kick … what is side-kick?'

'That Romanian, Ion.' She now felt irritated. 'Remember, the one who discovered the body?'

He looked flustered. 'Ah … him. He sleeps just behind the hotel by the wood store.' This she knew but let him continue. 'There's a room where the summer casual workers sleep. At the moment he's the only one that uses it. Always during the day he is in the hotel or at the Beachcomber. He usually sleeps during the morning because he's out most of the night with Petra.' He shrugged his shoulders. 'Or whenever he drinks too much and that's why he didn't go with Petra that night. He was drunk.'

'Or so he said,' she snapped back. She continued, 'so he could be in his room during the day time but normally out with Petra at night?'

He touched his cap and watched as she walked back to the hotel; he found her feisty spirit very attractive. He looked up at the sky and then studied the swell of the sea with the white horses starting to split the dark grey water, *no it's too quiet, nothing will happen tonight*, and then recalling his father's counsel, *nothing comes from nothing*.

At dinner that evening, she watched as Petra and Ion left to go to Ingissy and prepare for the night's fishing. Earlier they had been arguing in the bar and Kelena had to shout at them. They sulked and sat each end of the bar with their backs to each other, reminding Sarah of the painting in her child's bedroom of two African children either end of a log, titled, *The Tiff*. She grinned at Geraldine as they eventually shuffled past without acknowledging the guests. Geraldine whispered across to Sarah, 'good riddance to them I say. Don't know why she doesn't kick *him* out. I would.' Harold rolled his eyes at Sarah from behind his paper.

Geraldine's *mister creepy* and his companion Danni were in the far corner of the bar. They were joined by three new German couples that evening. The hotels were also starting to fill with Greek casuals for the approaching holiday weekend; the Beachcomber opposite was beginning to get noisy as a wedding party arrived; cars and mopeds parking on any available waste ground. Sarah slipped away to her room and changed into a dark T-shirt and shorts, pulling on gloves. She pushed the Beretta into her waistband, switched on the television, turning up the volume and silently left her room. She looked into the empty reception and lifted the wood store key from the panel.

On the island called Ingissi, Henry carried a rubbish bag and walked the guard dog over the wooden bridge to the concrete jetty triggering the sensor to floodlight the area. He threw the day's rubbish into the skip with a flourish of his arm, a performance he had enacted every night since arriving on the island. He watched the last but one of the fishing boats heading out of the harbour to anchor one mile off shore, as they had probably done for centuries. One boat remained tied up, its diesel engine ticking over, the air fumy. The two men standing in the boat were arguing. He recognised the dark, swarthy fisherman who was waving his arms and shouting at the other man who he had only recently seen; probably a casual seasonal help. He was slightly built; wearing a baseball cap pulled down and appeared to be drunk. He jumped from the boat onto the jetty and staggered, just stopping himself from falling into the water. He lurched over to one of the pickups and fell in slamming the door. The fisherman jumped from the boat and ran after him, but he was too late as it shot forward, just missing him and disappearing up the hill leading in the direction of the town. The fisherman shouted and waved his fist in the air before untying the mooring-rope and climbing angrily back into his boat. The boat reversed away, swinging round and heading out to sea causing waves to splash against the jetty.

Henry grinned and called the dog over, having enjoyed his unexpected evening's entertainment and slowly continued his customary doggy-walk through the woods.

A crescent moon created a surrealistic icy colour as Sarah's shadowy figure dropped down from the wall separating the hotel from the wood store. She twisted the key, its sudden sharp click drowned in laughter and music from the Beachcomber; trained reactions making her glance intently behind, assessing the situation. She gently pushed the door open to be greeted by a musty, damp smell. *How could anyone sleep in here? No wonder he looks chalky.* The beam from her torch swept around the dark interior of the Romanian's room; she was surprised at its tidiness, the bed neatly made, his clothes hanging from a rod that had been improvised by jamming it between a shelf and a tall bookcase On a bedside table stood a half-empty whisky bottle; 'maybe that's what they were arguing about?' she muttered quietly as she rummaged through the single drawer, but found only personal items. On the shelf were stacked several books with titles she assumed were in Romanian. She ran her fingers along and pulled out a dark, leather bound, medieval looking Romanian Bible with an embossed gold cross in the centre of the cover. She unclipped the heavy brass clasp holding the covers together. The hollowed out inside had a small black handgun set into soft moulded foam; Kolibri-Kopi engraved on the handle. *Why do they always choose bibles?* ran through her mind. A small container was set within the foam. She unscrewed the container lid to reveal the tiny, uranium dart shaped ammunition. She removed one and slipped it into her pocket. Suddenly the sound of a revving engine came over the crazy, sonorous thump-thump of music from the Beachcomber. She heard approaching footsteps. She had just snapped shut the bible clasp as the door crashed open behind her and the light flicked on.

She swung round dazzled by the sudden glare of the naked bulb just above her head, staring into the insane and dense red eyes of the Romanian. He sent out a high pitched howl and lunged forward. At the same time she heard a crack, and a blinding orange flash caught her eyes in a sulphuric smell, a sudden burning in her side made her gasp. She felt his arm yank round her neck and the acrid odour of whisky overpowering. Her immediate reaction brought her knee up and he buckled and loosened his grip. She grabbed his head and kicked his legs away. He dropped like a sack of bones with his skull banging down on the tiled floor; the cracking of his neck was as sharp and sudden as the gun he had just fired.

She kicked the door shut and slumped to the floor trying to control her breathing. She screamed, 'DAMN ... DAMN.' Her focus distorted with racing lights, her eyes smarting and running. Suddenly she could feel warmth trickling down her side. She wiped her tears away and pulled up her shirt. Blood had started to ooze from a small wound under her arm. She sighed with relief; her smarting eyes making out merely a flesh wound.

She placed her fingers on his neck, although it was obvious he was dead. She shuddered at the sight of those blank, staring hellish eyes. 'DAMN.' She had blown it. *What the hell was he doing back here?* The thump-thump of the wild music seemed to be getting louder, pounding round the room and penetrating into her head, its violence swamping her senses. She controlled herself by breathing slowly, she calmed down, her eyes now focused again. She went through his trouser pockets; *coins, drachma notes, some Romanian – maybe?* A flap in the back of a wallet held a small slip of paper with telephone numbers and scrawled names. She put the paper in her pocket and slipped the wallet back into his trousers. She eased the pistol from his grip and pushing it into in her waist band. She tried another pocket and a small plastic packet touched her fingers, out rose the sweet pungent smell of heroin. She hesitated but quickly slipped it into her pocket. The infernal thumping continued to make her head spin, and the wound burning like a hot poker in her side made her feel sick. Pulling a tissue from her pocket she pressed it hard against the stinging pain to stop the trickle of blood. She moved across to turn off the light. In the outside world the sudden violence had gone unnoticed and life was continuing its crazy zombie dance. She cautiously re-opened the door to lean against the heavy wooden frame, staring at Petra's pickup, its door open, the engine still ticking over, standing alone in the moonlight. She was thinking ... thinking fast and trying to reason, clear and straight ... *the telephone booth!*

She turned off the engine and went back to the body and took the coins from his pocket. Holding her side she kept in the shadows when passing the Beachcomber and headed to the lone telephone booth. She opened the door to a rancid smell of sick and beer, causing nausea to rise up in her throat.

'Is that you Ricki?'

His voice changed as he recognised her and curious at her tone. 'Hi, how are things?'

'Ricki, I need your help. Now ... it's urgent.'

'Where are you?'

'I'm at the rear of the Hotel Mira ... where I'm staying ... just by the church.'

'What, opposite the Beachcomber?'

'Yes,' she snapped, 'I'll flash my torch.'

'I'll be there in about thirty minutes.' He paused. 'Can't you get Panos?'

'No. Not this time. Just keep out of his way. And Ricki, do you have a first-aid kit handy?'

'Sure, but why?'

'Just bring it,' she shouted. She pushed open the door gulping in the fresh air and was immediately sick; adding to her misery. A passing couple ignored her as yet another over indulgent holiday maker and went into the Beachcomber. She hurried back to the wood store, keeping within the dusky shadows, well away from the moonlight.

On the shelf she noticed a pile of fresh sheets and pillowcases. Tearing a case into a makeshift bandage she tied it tight around her body. *God, it was sore!*

His timing was good; thirty minutes later an old Escort pulled into a side track next to the hotel. The headlights turned off further back along the road. She noticed the interior light had also been turned off as Ricki opened the door ... she couldn't help thinking, *he's remembering his training*! The engine noise had been drowned out with that infernal thump-thump from the wedding party. Sarah flashed her torch and he approached with his figure at first silhouetted by the moonlight, and then disappearing into the shadows.

'In here,' she whispered. Closing the door she switched on the light.

'What the hell?' He knelt down and put his fingers on the neck. 'Hey, I've seen him with the fishermen.'

'He's our killer, called Ion.'

Sarah quickly filled him in with the events of the past hour. He gave her a strange look. 'That's how you treated me. Remember? That could have been my neck.'

'Yes. But you weren't trying to kill me ... or were you?

'What happens now? Shouldn't we get Panos?

'No! There's no sign of injury except where his head hit the floor.'

He studied the body and agreed. She continued, 'so this is what we must do.' Her plan had him nodding.

Ricki drove Petra's pickup through the town and up the hill before pulling alongside the Santa Maria chapel. The silver moonlight broken by high scudding clouds caused strange and sudden dancing shadows, making the scene surreal as the two figures struggled to carry the body from the back of the pickup to the cliff edge; Sarah feeling weak and still nausea. Ricki noticed his companion's heavy breathing as she picked up each hand and scraped the soil into the nails. 'Ready?' she whispered. He nodded and the body slid over the edge taking gravel and rocks down. They heard the dull thud and falling debris as it bounced against the cliff side ... and then just the sound of the sea lapping against the shore below. She threw the Romanian's baseball cap into the darkness. The distant thump-thump cries of the wedding party floating up like echoing waves from the illuminated town far below. Sarah felt tired and giddy and he put his arm around her as she swayed. She gasped and jerked away clasping her side; he looked at his hand which was warm and shiny in the moonlight. 'My God, you're injured. Is that why you asked for the first-aid?'

She nodded. 'I'm OK. Luckily it's only a flesh wound. I must sit down.' He gently lowered her onto the cliff embankment, the perspiration starting to run down the small of her back, her hands shaking. 'First there are things we need to do.' She pulled the heroin from her pocket and gave it to him. 'Get the whisky

48

bottle from the pickup and lay the heroin on the cliff edge with the whisky bottle on its side ... and take the top off.'

She watched his moonlit figure but her thoughts were dulled, just wishing she could be anywhere, just anywhere away from that damned infernal row coming up from the laughing town below. He came back and sat beside her, both staring across the cliff edge into the darkness, the deed done and both deep in their separate thoughts.

Ricki broke the silence. 'We must get you looked at. Are you able to walk down the hill ... or shall I get the Escort?'

'We'll walk,' and as she stood up she became aware of the miniature statue of Santa Maria looking down on her. In the dull light the figurine seemed to be floating in an alcove set in the side of the chapel; the moon casting its cold and silver light across the saint's questioning face. Sarah felt those dark eyes probing deep into her soul; approval or condemnation? She felt a wave of numbness sweep up her body; she felt troubled. She hesitated and made the sign of the cross before they slowly wound their way back down into town, his arm firmly supportive around her; at that moment she needed his warmth and all his strength. What a complete mess she'd made of the evening. Janus won't be pleased.

The lonely pickup abandoned in the moonlight, the driver's door purposely left open, keys in the ignition, the subdued orange glow from the radio spluttering its flow of nightly inane chatter, and the sudden high-pitched wail of Denis Rousso's *Forever and Ever* offending the night air. Far out to sea, the carnival lights of a ghostly cruise liner slipped through the inky night; unaware of the Greek tragedy unfolding two miles away on a small turtle-shaped holiday island called Petromos.

'... come old friend, for soon doth part'

Sarah replaced the keys back in the reception and led Ricki up to her room. He opened the first-aid bag and she hesitated before making a conscience attempt to remove her top.

'For Christ sake woman let me take it off. How can I clean you up?' He pulled it over her head, dropping the blood soaked garment to the floor. He went into the shower room and ran a sink of warm water. He carefully unwound the pillowcase bandage and they both examined the wound. 'I think you'll live Sarah. At least it's stopped bleeding.'

He cleansed the wound with a disinfectant and left her to wash her front. She became aware of his gentleness as he dressed the injury and found herself watching his face showing concern. She frowned as he expertly cut a plaster into thin strips, and winched as he used the strips to pull the wound together, before winding a bandage around her body. She smiled her thanks at him.

'You should have been a doctor, or a nurse.'

'I did first aid with St. John's,' was his explanation, 'comes in useful sometimes. Although usually at rugby matches and big hairy brutes, not young ladies.'

She swigged down some pain killers and finished the rest of the water not wanting to hear the end of his sentence. 'God I was thirsty.'

'You say the flash caught your face?' She nodded. 'Let me check your eyes.' He held her face, finding himself willingly submerged in the extraordinary depth and colour of her pupils; he quickly swallowed. 'You've a slight burn to one side of your cheek. Looks as though you been in the sun. Your pupils seem OK. Better get checked out when you get back home.' He couldn't help holding her face as she started to blush and bit her lower lip; memories came flooding back from her childhood; she remembered *his* boyish features, *he* held her face, *he* had also been mesmerised by those eyes and tried to kiss her; but she had screamed and run away; childhood games. There was an awkward pause and he let go.

Ricki felt strangely disturbed in that revealing moment and turned away to gather up the makeshift bandage and her bloodied shirt. 'I'll drop these in the waste on my way out.' He glanced at her again. 'You gonna be OK?'

She nodded.

'Better get a doctor to see that wound. We don't want any infection setting in. I suggest you wear a loose blouse tomorrow and take it easy. If anybody queries anything, say you tore a muscle in your side.'

He noticed her look. 'Oh dear, not doing very well, am I ma'am?'

She shook her head and said sharply, 'don't teach me my job.' The sharp rejoinder made him pause. His face dropped; that camaraderie they had enjoyed over the past hour suddenly vanished; she was his boss, the social tier was back.

His turn to blush and he moved to leave. 'I'll see what I can do about a medic. Can't use the local doc, I'll contact the embassy ... if that's OK with you?'

She nodded. 'Please. Tomorrow's going to be interesting day, so let's hope it works otherwise there'll be hell to play.'

He opened the door and turned. 'I'll get back to you first thing in the morning, ma'am. Hope you manage to sleep well.'

She nodded and suddenly moved over to him putting her hand on his arm. 'Thanks Ricki. It's greatly appreciated.' She didn't really want to be on her own, she wasn't as independent as she tried to tell herself. She suddenly leaned forward and kissed him on the cheek; *he didn't run away.*

His eyes gleamed. 'Does that mean I'm back in your good books and you won't be sending me to Russia?'

She was tired and tried to laugh. 'There never was a posting for Russia.'

'Damn! And I've already bought some snow boots.'

She closed the door, and leaned against the wall feeling emotionally and physically drained. She took another swig of water and sat on the bed. Easing herself round and holding her side, she slowly sank back closing her eyes, and as she slipped into a thankful sleep, she felt pleasurable warmth thinking of him holding her face. She wished she hadn't been so sharp with him earlier. He was only trying to reassure her; or was it because she had to admit she was finding herself drawn and didn't want to acknowledge her weakness; her usual reaction. She knew he had been taken in by her eyes. *He's arrogant blast him.* She softly drifted, *wonder why the name Ricki? I don't even know his real name?*

Geraldine remained sitting in the dark sipping her holiday gin and lemonade, having earlier enjoyed the last moment of the sun sinking towards the promise of another good tomorrow; the sunset so red it seemed about to burst into flames; the balcony air full of scent and warmth and husband Harold in bed catching up with his airport novel. From her balcony Geraldine thought she could hear voices coming from the young English woman's room. *Probably got the television on?* It suddenly went quiet and her sharp eyes became aware of a man's figure, just catching the moonlight, silently moving down the steps out of the darkness leading away from her room. Her eyes lit up and she rubbed her hands together with glee. 'Oh I do enjoy holiday romances,' she whispered, 'you never know what is going to happen next ... I wonder if he's Greek.' She stood up excited and hurried into their bedroom, 'Harold you'll never guess ...' Harold prejudged her and closed his eyes before she'd even entered.

Gradually she became aware of strong, argumentative Greek

voices with the occasional swearing; Kelena's high nasal pitch, and Petra with his low, whiney staccato groan. She slowly came round, staring at the ceiling. She caught the name Ion several times and the 'pickup missing'. Her head throbbed and she had a job to take it in, her mind still muddled and her body feeling as if she had been in a wrestling bout. Her eyes blinking and slowly focusing onto the early morning sun that streaked through a gap in the closed curtains; she watched in fascination as a spider skipped across the ceiling. Oh, how she could stay there all day and bury her face into the soft warmth of the pillow. She forgot and jerked as she rubbed her sore eye and tried to focus on the time. Her watch said eight. *Hell. I must go down at my regular time, all part of the damn act. Surprised Ricki didn't remind me to do that.* A few years ago she revelled in her work, but now ... questions she didn't have answers for. She slowly pulled the sheet away and tried to swing her legs over to the floor. She was stiff. Slowly she came to and reached for the pain-killers, aware the voices had gone. She stood up unsteady and walked stiffly to pull the curtains. The sharp sun hit her and she held a hand to shade her narrowed eyes. The right eye still felt sore. She looked in the mirror. She could still picture Ricki's face, looking into her eyes and still felt his strong hands holding her face. She had found that somehow disturbing and she had felt breathless, the memory strangely made her angry. She turned quickly away from the mirror. *What's going to greet me downstairs? Wonder if they've found the body yet?*

She slowly walked through the bar and onto the terrace with its early morning heady perfume from the colourful Pelargonium, her aches becoming easier as the painkillers started to kick in with every step. She tried to make her walk normal but there was no hiding her stiffness. Kelena was laying the tables, Sarah noting she was the first in. She looked up and smiled. 'Good morning Sarah. Oh dear you look stiff?'

Sarah nodded. 'Good morning Kelena. I must have pulled a muscle in my side.'

Kelena pulled a chair out and her face showed concern. 'Please come and sit down. Do you have any tablets?'

Sarah nodded. 'Yes thank you. But I could do with a strong black coffee please.'

As Kelena prepared the coffee, Sarah gently probed, calling into the bar, 'I woke early this morning by a couple arguing below my balcony. I think they were Greek.'

Kelena came back with two coffees and sat down. 'I'm so sorry my dear. That must have been Petra and me. Just as well you don't understand Greek. There was lots of swearing, mostly from me.'

'Oh dear ... a domestic tiff?'

'No. Ion has disappeared.'

'Disappeared?'

'Last night Petra wouldn't take him fishing because he was drunk. That's what the argument was about yesterday. They continued to argue at the fishing port, and he jumped in Petra's pickup and drove away. Petra assumed he would be there in the morning after he'd slept it off. It has happened before ... many times. He has to bring his fish back early to catch the first ferry to Piraeus ... very important. One of the other fishermen had to bring him back. On the way they found the pickup parked up by Santa Maria. No sign of him. Door open: keys in the ignition: the radio blaring out: no sign of Ion.' She raised her voice in anger, 'hope he's gone forever. Why Petra hangs around with him I don't know. Never did like him. He is mentally sick, up here.' She wiggled her finger to her forehead. 'That's what the shouting was about ... as if I had something to do with it!' She shrugged her shoulders, her voice rising, 'hope he's fallen over the cliff.'

Sarah tried to look shocked. 'He probably walked into the woods and is sleeping it off.'

She flicked her fingers. 'They found an empty bottle of whisky, and what I've always suspected.'

'Oh. What's that then?'

'They found drugs with the whisky. Mad. They are all mad. Make me angry.' She banged her head with her hand. 'Crazy. Sarah

I am so sorry, you are a guest here and you do not want to hear this sort of thing. You are a good woman and I don't suppose you ever come across bad people like that? I'm so sorry. Let me get you some breakfast. You must be hungry.' She made to go away but stopped. 'Oh, somebody called Ricki rang. Your cousin he says.' She laughed. 'You are very popular young lady Sarah. I am pleased for you. He asked to speak with you and said he would call in one hour.' She looked at her watch and confirmed to herself. 'About one hour ago. So if the phone rings, please answer as it will be him.' She nodded to herself. 'I think so. I'm now getting your breakfast. No more talking eh.' With that she disappeared into the kitchen.

'So far, so good,' mused Sarah Athina-Beaumont, the shrill ring from the reception phone making her jump.

She picked up the receiver. 'Hotel Mira.'

'Ah. I think I recognise the voice of my cousin Sarah ... correct?'

'Ricki I assume?'

'Of course! Who else? How are you?'

'I'm fine thank you.' Raising her voice to be overheard. 'Pulled a muscle in my side last night but it's OK. Bit sore today.'

'Are you having a quiet time ... no commotion?'

'Very quiet here. Apparently there's a Romanian workman gone missing and they've found the hotel pickup somewhere out of town near the cliff edge. Hotel owner's not very happy as you can imagine.'

'Still, it's not your problem. Oh by the way, a doctor friend of Uncle Alec is coming over on the early morning ferry. Perhaps you could go down and meet him. I know he will be pleased to see you. He can't stay long but thought he'd pop over as you know what Uncle Alec is like, he's always concerned about the well-being of his favourite niece.'

She caught the slight inflection intended to taunt her. *So he thinks that does he?*

'How will I know him?'

'Oh I think he'll pick you out, I gave him your description. He goes by the name of Phillip Makris ... Doctor Philip Makris.

He's also the embassy doctor, so you'll be in good hands. He understands the situation. Well, better get on I suppose. Take care.'

She frowned. 'Did you say Phillip Makris?'

'Yes. Mean anything to you?'

'No ...' She narrowed her eyes, thinking ... *can't be, not Doctor ... Phillip Makris?*

'Oh by the way ... I didn't realise what unusual eyes you have ... bye.'

She slowly replaced the receiver and grinned, pausing as she caught her reflection in a mirror. She examined her face, and then her eyes; she had always been aware of the effect they had on the men in her life. The door opened, and Geraldine with husband Harold in tow, entered and nodded, together with their cheerful 'good mornings'. Geraldine giving her a knowing look, with what Sarah thought, was a wink.

The early morning azure sky was awake, painting a view for the day ahead. The young English woman sat on a wooden crate watching the ferry backing in; the blast of its siren bouncing off the hills, its large ramp already starting to lower. Panos was busy ticking a clipboard and checking a pile of crates containing clucking and protesting chickens; a low loader waiting, its diesel throbbing, piled high with several steel skips waiting to take away the island's daily rubbish back to Piraeus, several cars and small trucks anxious to board, entire families of tourists eager to be off to the neighbouring island for the day. He occasionally glanced over to admire her; the typical English tourist with her wide brim straw bonnet, large sunglasses, matching loose cream blouse and skirt, her long slim legs shiny and golden in the early morning sun. He still couldn't take in that this slip of a girl had overpowered the bodyguard Ricki on Ingissi. Thoughts ran through his mind; *wonder who she is waiting for...? She wouldn't normally come down here ... strange about that Ion ...wonder if he did slip over the edge...?* Petra insisted he had tried to look over the edge ... *difficult to see of course ... I'll get him to bring his boat round when I've finished and we'll go and look from the sea.*

Soon there came the usual shouting; the iron scraping on concrete; the signal for engines to burst into life and the awaiting passengers fighting to board against those trying to disembark. Panos noticed she was now standing and studying the crowd walking from the ferry. Suddenly a young man, smartly dressed in cream slacks and a blue short-sleeved shirt, red bow tie and sporting a Panama hat remained looking around. He carried a small case, a newspaper under one arm and a small bunch of flowers. He spotted her and hesitated before walking across. He raised his hat in greeting and they shook hands, stood talking for a few minutes, when she suddenly flung her arms around him and they laughed and kissed like lovers. They walked away excited, chatting and smiling, she had her arm through his, staring into his face. Panos pulled a face and watched, feeling a twinge of jealousy.

'Oh Philip I can't believe this ... Doctor Philip Makris ... how wonderful. I was only thinking of you recently.' She laughed excitedly. 'Do you remember how we would play doctors and patients, and here you are, a real doctor. Wait till I tell my parents.'

He paused. 'And how are momma and poppa ...?'

'They're fine. Retired to Devon now ... into gardening.'

'... and Michael?'

'... a policeman. Detective Chief inspector would you believe!'

'Gosh. He's doing well. But are you on holiday here, Katie?'

She looked puzzled and frowned. 'Why do you ask?'

'But why else would you be here ... or do you live here?'

'Phillip you know you're not supposed to ask questions and please don't call me Katie.'

He stopped, feeling in his pocket. 'This is all so confusing.' He glanced at a piece of paper. 'I'm to meet a Sarah Athina-Beaumont here.' He glanced around.

She pulled him over to the parapet wall and they sat down. 'Phillip, that's me.'

'You ... but?'

She smiled and nodded. 'I was told a Doctor Phillip Makris would be coming over, and there are so many Phillips and Makris in Greece I didn't connect, especially ...' She emphasised, '*Doctor.*'

He offered the flowers, puzzled. 'Then these are for you Katie.'

'So this was for another woman then?'

He grinned. 'Yes, for a Miss Sarah Athina-Beaumont.' He glanced again at the paper. 'Going on the description given by ... Ricki? Yes, I see what he means.'

She tried to grab the paper. 'Let me see.'

He raised it up away above her head. 'Oh no young lady! My memory of a little girl called Katie Simpson is of a gawky tom-boy, with braces on her teeth and spindle legs. But now look at you ...' He didn't finish but grinned.

She blushed and looked away for a moment. 'You always were the flatterer, Phillip Makris.'

He chuckled. 'Well you're not reading this Miss Katie, and there's no doubt you have made an impression on this ... Ricki, or am I reading more into this?'

'You're reading much too much Phillip. He actually works for me. I'm his boss out here, or *ma'am* as he likes to call me.'

His face clouded. 'What are you involved in Katie? Why couldn't you see the local doctor and what exactly happened? Where is this injury?'

She stood up. 'Look Phillip, you mustn't ask questions. And only refer to me as Sarah, please. For appearances I'm having a few days break from London. Getting some sun and ... I do not speak Greek so please only in English.' She laughed and shook her head. 'Comes in useful sometimes though. Come on, let's go to the hotel and have a coffee and then you better look at my injury.' She held her hand on her side. 'It's here. It seems to be OK, but very sore.'

'This injury concerns me Kat ... sorry ... Sarah. I don't think I'll get used to calling you Sarah. Let me get this right ... someone shot at you ... is that correct?'

'Don't ask Phillip. Don't ask too many questions, please. Remember this is embassy business.'

They continued out of the port and he glanced over to Panos. 'That policeman seems very interested in us.'

She smiled. 'I think he's jealous. Thinks he's the island Romeo. He doesn't like strangers moving on to his territory!'

'Oh it's like that,' he murmured with a chuckle.

'No it's not like that ... doctor.'

He noticed her bristle. 'In some ways you haven't changed have you? Come on, I'm dying for a drink.'

Doctor Phillip Makris studied his childhood friend across the table as they sat under the olive tree. Goodness knows how many years had passed and now the memories came flooding back in waves. They had lived next door to each other in Athens and the two families became very close. In fact Phillip was like a sibling to the two. He was older and very protective of Katie. When they moved back to the UK there were the usual promises of keeping in touch, but as the years passed, the cards and letters started to drop off as they went their separate ways and made their new lives and new friends. It was so wonderful to see her again and what a difference in her. *But what is she involved in? Obviously government work as it involves the embassy. Being here with another name ... she's not going to tell me of course.*

'You look very distinguish Phillip. Love the moustache, it suits you.'

He grinned and run his finger across. 'Why thank you. I did think of shaving it off, but as you approve, then I will leave it on.'

'I sat in the Oddessa bar and looked up at the Acropolis and thought of when we used to play hide and seek amongst the lumps of Marble. Then we'd get chased off by some official.'

He nodded. 'Yes, and then you would disappear but I always knew where to find you ...'

In unison they both grinned and said, '... in the Parthenon.'

He shook his head. 'Your mother always said that was your second home; you always were a crazy girl and I think maybe you still are. But we wouldn't be able to do that today of course. You can't just stroll in there now; such a shame. Haven't been up there for years ... I've been reluctant because I want to remember it as it was. To see it now would spoil those super years we had.'

She nodded in agreement. 'And then yesterday I stood at the top of the Ploutarchou steps. Remember how we would run up all those thousands of steps? Well it seemed like thousands, couldn't do it now.'

'Guess who always reached the top first?'

'Definitely wasn't going to let boys beat me.'

He looked thoughtfully at her. 'I imagine nothing has changed.'

She nodded. 'Guess you're right Phillip. There are times it has stood me in good stead. Well, tell me about yourself.' She hesitantly glanced at the ring on his wedding finger. 'I see you're married.'

He nodded. 'Yes. Her name is Elissa and we have one boy Jerome, and one girl Helen.' He pulled out his wallet and handed her a photo of the three.

'Oh Phillip. How wonderful! Your Elissa is lovely and the children are gorgeous. What a lucky fella you are.'

'Yes I'm very proud of my family.' He looked at her ring-less finger and frowned. 'No love in your life?'

She shook her head. 'Nothing like that. Probably just as well.'

He leaned across and laid his hand on hers. 'Don't leave it too late Katie; there are more important things in life than work. The years are passing so fast and just think, out there, somewhere, there is someone who would love to make you happy.' He squeezed her hand '... promise?'

She smiled and nodded. 'I promise. Is that my doctor's advice, or orders?'

'No! Just an old friend.' He looked at his watch. 'I think we should have a look at your injury. Where can we go?'

'Up to my room, they should have finished cleaning by now.'

Kelena came in on cue. 'Would you two like another coffee?'

'No thank you Kelena. I'd like to show Phillip the view from my balcony and we have so much to chat about.' She smiled at him. 'Old times, eh Phillip?'

Kelena took the flowers. 'I'll put these in a vase and leave them on your table.'

Sarah handed the family photo to Kelena. 'Hasn't he got a lovely family Kelena?'

Her eyes lit up and agreed. She smiled at Sarah. 'The other day, what I said about Greek men, they're not all like Petra ... thank god.'

Sarah laughed and looked at her watch. 'Can you stay for lunch Phillip? There's plenty of time before the afternoon ferry.'

'Of course, I'd love that, Katie.'

Kelena frowned - *Katie*, but she ignored it by nodding. 'No problem, I'll lay your table for two then.'

She watched the two leave the bar; the young English woman noticeably different, happy to be with her friend. She smelt the flowers and arranged them in a vase. 'No, not all Greek men are like my Petra,' she muttered to herself. She made the sign of the cross looking thoughtful. *Why did he call her Katie?*

Just then Petra and Panos entered. Petra went straight to the bar and poured out two glasses of Metaxa. He looked drawn and pale beneath his weather-beaten face, and visibly shaking. He handed one to Panos and swigged the brandy straight down. Kelena stood with her arms folded. Petra stared at the counter, moving his head slowly side to side, his shoulders drooped. Panos slowly sipped his brandy and turned to glance at Kelena. He moved over to her.

'It's Ion.'

'Oh. What about Ion?'

'He's dead.'

She stared at him and crossed herself. 'Well, is that all you have to say?' She gestured. 'How is he dead? Explain.'

He shrugged his shoulders, glanced at Petra, then back to her. 'We found him at the foot of the cliff. Just below the chapel. He must have slipped over. We know he was drunk last night, and there was an empty whisky bottle by the pickup, with what looks like drugs. I reckon he was going to smoke it but slipped over. Crazy fool. He knew it was dangerous up there.'

She felt shaky with the news and tried to concentrate on the tables but suddenly turning to Petra shaking her fist with anger. 'I told you he was trouble. Never did like him. There was something creepy about him. Why you let him work with you, I never know.'

Petra shouted back, 'what's that got to do with him being dead.'

She tossed her head and glared with merciless eyes. 'Everything!' she cried and carried the tray into the kitchen.

Petra croaked, 'What happens now then Panos?'

'I'll have to let the mainland police know. They'll send somebody over from Piraeus to collect him and make a report. You'll have to make a statement. It's straight forward. Pity the island doctor's visit isn't until tomorrow, I'd like to get the death certificate written out so they can come and get the body off the island.'

The island policeman didn't like a casual thing like death to interfere with his daily routine.

'...the wound doth cut her heart'

They lingered for a moment on the balcony; she slipped her arm tightly through his trying to identify the various islands. She then pointed further east. 'As far as I can make out, that is Piraeus and that dip should be the Corinth Canal.'

Phillip squeezed her arm. 'Hey, do you remember when we took that canoe along the canal and got into trouble? Our parents went mad. Banned from canoeing! Well not for long thank goodness.'

A familiar voice called out, 'hello ... hello!'

'Oh no,' groaned Sarah, and smiled as she turned and saw Geraldine waving from her balcony; she wanted to stay there forever holding his arm, but she waved back and whispered, 'let's go inside Phillip, I thought they were out.'

'Like that, is it?' He chuckled as they moved back into the room.

'Yes. She'll make something of you being here.'

'Keep them guessing. Makes her holiday I expect.' He opened his case. 'Right Katie ... I can call you Katie in here surely. Let's have a look.'

She started to remove her blouse. He appeared awkward.

'What's the problem Phillip?'

'Katie, I find this difficult.'

'Why?'

'I know it's crazy, and yes, I should be used to this, but ... you're Katie, my dear friend.'

'Does it embarrass you?'

'Well, yes. Somehow it doesn't seem right.'

'Oh Philip, remember, we used to go skinny dipping?'

'I know, but, well you're a grown woman now.'

'Do we have a choice? I've got to have it looked at.'

'Yes of course. I'm sorry. I'm being silly. Well as long as you don't mind?'

'Get on with it Phillip,' she said with a grin and with that she slipped the blouse off and unclipped her bra.

He carefully unwound the bandage. 'Whoever did this made a good job of it.' He frowned. 'Was it Ricki?'

She nodded. 'He wasn't embarrassed, but I was.'

'I bet he wasn't,' he said quietly. 'He did a good job though.' He lifted the dressing away and she jumped as it stuck. 'Sorry. It looks good. No infections thank goodness. It doesn't need any stitches. He's managed to pull the wound together with the plaster. Very clever. Excellent! You must pass my comments on to him. When you get home have it checked out ... you will have a scar I'm afraid.'

She pulled a face. 'Ah well, a memento of my Greek holiday.'

He took a closer look. 'Oh Katie you were lucky, another few millimetres ...' he didn't continue. 'Hope this isn't an everyday occurrence in your work?'

She shook her head. 'No. Lots of bruises though.'

'I can see why you couldn't go to a doctor. He would have to report a bullet wound.' He grimaced. 'It doesn't surprise me you do this work. Always the tom-boy was my Katie!'

'So you said before. Puts an end to my swimming on this supposed holiday?'

'No. It would do it good. If you wear a loose top nobody will see the dressing and you can always say you've had too much sun. You won't need the bandage, just the dressing.'

He clipped her bra and helped her on with the blouse. He rummaged in his case and handed her a small bottle. 'These pain killers are better than those others. Take some now. There's no sign of infection but take one of these others for five days, just in case, and you must have it checked out back in London. Promise?'

She nodded and swigged them down with water. 'Yes doctor.'

'Now let me look at those eyes. I understand you were blinded for a moment. Follow my pen.' She watched the moving pen and he felt once again the strange intensity of her pupils. He whispered, 'your eyes haven't changed have they? How many hearts have been broken, Katie Simpson?' He suddenly held her face, his eyes suddenly twinkled. 'Do you remember when I held you like this and I tried to ... and you got angry?'

'Well I was a young girl then, and wasn't I silly? Who would have believed all these years later we would still be playing doctors and patients, I should run away now, doctor.' She grinned and kissed him. Then she remembered a few hours ago she killed a man and her mask dropped, Phillip noticed, and they were back in the present time; he repacked his case.

'Oh Katie, I was asked to give you this, something from,' he frowned, 'Uncle Alec?' She took the envelope and put it in her bag.

About the same time on Ingissi, Johnnie carefully picked his way down the garden path, noticeably unsteady, looking for Ricki who was assembling an umbrella for Henry's wife Rose. It was the shadiest part of the garden, always with a slight welcome breeze. Rose did not like the heat, or the quietness, and longed for the coolness of London with all the noise and bustle of the East End. Ricki grew up near to where she was born, and so they had an affinity. She liked him but found him a little full of himself, and Henry's account of the way that young woman had him on the floor made her say, 'Well it won't do him any "arm and she went into her kitchen chuckling.

'Ah Ricki,' Johnnie rasped, flicking ash from his stomach as it dropped from his cigarette. 'Ricki! I've got visitors coming this evening for a meal about eight. Just some acquaintances I met in town when you last allowed me out,' he growled, picking his words carefully with noted sarcasm, cheap whisky oozing from his sweat. 'They're OK, just coming in for a drink. Don't want you frisking them. They want to see my paintings. Apparently they're art lovers.'

Ricki pursed his lips, free drinks more like it. He raised his eyebrows. 'Any idea what their names are? You know I have to make a note of all visitors.'

Johnnie shook his head. 'Can't remember ... Podolski? That's it ... Podolski ... stupid name these foreigners have. Shouldn't worry though, it's all unofficial. Perhaps you could keep out of the way. Wouldn't want them to think I've a gorilla minding me. Any case, Henry will be with me.' He winked. 'Lose yourself. Why don't you go into town like you did last night? Got a bird down there, 'ave yer? Here, go and give her a good time.' With that, he pulled a rolled wad of drachma notes from his shorts and stuffed some into Ricki's shirt pocket, turned and flicked his cigarette butt into the bushes.

Ricki watched him zigzag back with an unsteady sailor gait along the path. *So he noticed my going. At least he thinks it was a girl. Well it was of course. Wonder if the body has been found yet?* He still felt the stiffness in his shoulder from his first encounter with her. *That Romanian didn't stand a chance; didn't know what he was letting himself in for. Wonder what Johnnie's up to? Don't trust him. Think I'll give her a bell.*

He counted the money.

Christ, he does want me out the way! She'll have to let me buy her a drink now ... it's official!

'... memories, but clinging cobwebs from times past'

Kelena met Sarah and Phillip walking down the stairs from her room. Sarah had her arm through his and Kelena thought how her eyes shone and her manner most girlish. She had looked pale this morning but now there was a delightful colour in her expression. She was giggling at something he had just said. Sarah's face dropped when she saw Kelena waiting.

'Sarah I've just had a call from,' Kelena glanced at Phillip, 'Ricki. He said would you call him, it is urgent.'

'I see. Thank you.'

Phillip nodded at her. 'Go ahead now. I'll wait on the terrace.'

Sarah looked anxiously at him. 'Sorry Phillip ... would you mind?'

He smiled at Kelena. 'I think a beer would go down a treat.'

As Kelena moved to go she looked at Sarah, her face troubled. 'About Ion ... I'll tell you when you've finished. Oh, he said something about a battery?' She turned and the doctor followed her into the bar.

Phillip thought Katie had looked tired and drawn on the jetty; that wound could have been worse. It had frightened her of course, despite her bravado; it had frightened him. She had perked up with their meeting and how wonderful to see her smile return and to meet up after all this time. He grinned and touched his moustache. 'So she approves.' He opened his Athens News as Kelena placed a beer on the table.

Sarah pressed the + terminal and a tiny red light glowed. She dialled and Ricki's voice answered, 'hi.'

'You wanted me to call you?'

'Yes. Are you using the battery? Can you hear a hum and the light on?'

'Yes! Get on with it Ricki,' she snapped.

'Johnnie informs me he's got visitors tonight and wants me out of the way. Says it's to see his paintings and have a meal. If that's true they can't have much taste ... the paintings I mean. And he gave me some money to give my girl a good time ... whoever she might be.'

She ignored his obvious drift. 'Any idea as to when they'll be arriving?

'Eight.'

'Any names?'

'Yeah. Foreign name ... Podolski.'

'Ah, that's interesting. He's staying at my hotel. I asked uncle if they had anything on him. Give me five minutes. I'll ring you back.'

She tore open the envelope Phillip had brought over from the embassy for her, unfolded the A4 sheet and scanned down the writing. She put her finger on a name -

Shumonko Podolski - born in the Ukraine; links with Romanian mafia ... Italian Mafia ... arms running ... drugs. Wanted by the French DGSE intelligence - Israel's Mossad ... M16 interested.

Ion- unsure - suspect he is the loose cannon assassin from Romania that's been cropping up this past year under different names.

Danni - *interesting as his details have been blanked out... wonder why?*

She grinned as she read -

Harold Percival Spencer ... retired bank manager ... interests: golf - bridge and steam railways.

Geraldine Daisy Bodmin Spencer ... retired headmistress ... councillor and chairperson of Southwick Action committee ... both living in Kent.

She glanced through the open window at her Phillip sitting in the shade under the tired olive tree reading his paper; she felt a lump in her throat and an overwhelming weariness; *at that moment she would gladly trade it all to share his life ... but he wasn't hers any more: they were grown up, not children.* She paused a moment before picking up the receiver to talk to Ricki.

'Our mister Podolski is an interesting man.' She read out his history and he gave a low whistle. She continued. 'I know he's buying a house here. That Ion is stated as unknown but suspected as a loose assassin. Not any more he's not.' She heard him chuckle and continued, 'strange about Podolski's companion Danni, his details have been blanked out? Our agent must have walked into something that's brewing and mistaken maybe for the opposition. Probably thought he was Russian. Oh yes, I have a feeling our friend from last night has been found.'

Phillip looked over the top of his paper and could just see her in the reception gloom through the open window. He watched her open the envelope he'd been entrusted with that morning by the young, long haired, fresh-faced man from the Business Attaché's security office; irritated at his insistence that he should hand it to her personally, or bring it straight back. Although she was now a woman, he still could see that tom-boy spirit in her. It was so nice to relive their childhood. *Why couldn't those days continue ... why do we have to grow up?* The thought of how near that bullet came caused him to pull a face and shake his head; *still getting into scrapes.*

Sarah closed her eyes, her mind covering all the possibilities. 'Have you got that bug I gave you?'

He was irritated. 'Yes!'

'How far would you say the cliffs are across from the island?'

'Cliffs?'

'Yes. The slope I climbed up when you watched me with your binoculars.'

He hesitated, caught out. 'I wasn't watching you.'

'I suppose you were bird watching,' she snapped.

She thought she heard him chuckle behind his reply. 'About half mile as the crow flies.'

"Then this is what we'll do .... I'll see you later ... and don't be late!" She replaced the receiver and turned to look out of the window.

Phillip became aware she had finished as she stood by the window looking across at him. She abruptly pulled away and came onto the terrace. He stood and pulled a chair for her and they sat down in the dappled shade with her looking at him without saying a word. He spoke at last, 'I know what you are thinking, Katie. You can't turn the clock back. We took different paths when we were young children; you went one way and I took another. My father always reminds me that it's not where you start your journey but how you finish. I think today our meeting has brought home what you are missing. You seem to have devoted your life to a career. Maybe it was a pity it was me who came to treat your wound?'

She shook her head. 'No Phillip, it's been so lovely to catch up again, and seeing the photo of your family has brought home to me what's been bothering me these past few months. I've been stubborn and dismissive of what my close friends have tried to tell me; Katie Simpson always knows best of course. I pretend not to see what is in the mirror. I've been frightened of any close relationship in case it interfered with my work.' She frowned, and then grinned dismissively, showing a slight embarrassment? 'In fact I think I have a reputation as the *ice virgin*. I should have let you kiss me when you held my face that time when we were children. Stupidly I ran away, and I suppose I've been running ever since. But then I couldn't, she had it all planned out for me, didn't she?' As if he would understand.

He didn't understand and ignored her last sentence. She had

always said strange things as a young girl and she hadn't changed even now as an adult. He noticed her eyes had a mist of tears. 'Please Katie. No regrets ... no regrets. Don't spoil the day.'

She cleared her throat and tried to smile, wiping her eyes with a tissue, leaning forward and resting her chin in her hand. 'Where's my beer Doctor?'

Kelena broke the moment coming onto the terrace bringing another beer to the table, discreetly ignoring Sarah's sad face.

Sarah looked up. 'You were going to tell me about Ion?'

'You are aware he went missing?' Kelena said.

Sarah nodded.

'His body was found at the bottom of the cliff this morning. Just below the Santa Maria chapel. He was drunk of course, and on drugs. He knew the danger up there.' She showed her anger. 'They are all idiots. Now he's gone.' She patted her chest. 'I won't miss him. I won't have him hanging around here anymore, drinking my Metaxa ... or feeding him.' She bristled and went back into the kitchen.

Phillip leaned back into his chair. 'What was all that about?'

Sarah was half way through explaining as Panos appeared, followed by Petra who slunk into the bar. Panos paused by their table and touched his cap and smiled at her. He turned to Philip. 'Good morning, I saw you arrive.' He indicated with his hand to both of them. 'You seem good friends, and any friend of this dear lady, is a friend of me ... mine. I am Panos the island policeman and anybody, or anything which comes onto the island I am responsible for.'

Phillip stood and they shook hands.

Sarah indicated Phillip with a warm smile. 'This is Doctor Makris who comes from Athens, we are old friends. He has come to spend a few hours with me. Talk over old times.'

'You are a medical Doctor?' Phillip frowned and nodded. Panos's eyes lit up. 'Ah maybe you could help? We have a problem. This morning we discovered the body of one of the foreigners who work on our island. He was drunk last night and must have slipped over the edge of the cliff on the road leading out of town. We found the pickup he was driving parked by the Chapel of Santa Maria.' He crossed himself. 'After the ferry had been in, I took a boat to look for him. We found him on the rocks directly below the Chapel; damage to the head of course. Do you practice in Athens?'

Phillip nodded. 'Has your local doctor seen him? It's very important when there's been an accident. The Examining Magistrate will need a report immediately.'

'We have no doctor here. A doctor comes over from the neighbouring island twice a week to hold a surgery. Anything more serious, then an available boat, or helicopter, would take that person straight to Piraeus.' He stroked his chin. 'Rather than wait for the doctor's return tomorrow, I wondered if you could make out the death certificate. It is a straight forward accident and I would like to get the body off the island with this afternoon's ferry.' He indicated up to the sky with his eyes and shrugged. 'In this heat ... we have no facilities here ... and as you know he has to be buried within four days.'

'I can do the certificate, but the Magistrate will need a report as the death is unnatural. As a policeman I'm sure you understand the rules concerning accidents.' He looked at his watch. 'This mustn't take long, I came particularly to see this young lady and I have to catch the ferry back.'

Panos agreed, nodding. 'Of course, but I could arrange for the high-speed twin-hull ferry to divert and pick you up later this afternoon. But if you can handle the certificate for me, I would be very grateful.' He turned to Sarah. 'Young lady, I am very sorry to take your friend away, but this is very important.'

She was unsure about Phillip getting involved but she smiled and put her hand on Phillip. 'Of course Panos, as long as you don't keep him too long.'

Phillip tried not to grin at her obvious dig at the island Romeo. He rose and pushed the *Athens News* across to her. 'Perhaps you would like to catch up with the big wide world.'

Panos raised his eyebrows. 'I didn't know you could read Greek, Miss?'

For a moment her eyes narrowed. 'I can always look at the pretty pictures.'

Phillip smiled at her reply. 'I'll just pop to the men's room. I won't be long.' He swilled the remainder of his beer down and strode off through the bar.

Panos sat in the vacant chair. 'I've searched the pockets and there's only a wallet with money.'

Sarah felt she had to be careful with how much detail she should confide with the island policeman. She offered, 'there's no doubt in my mind he's somehow involved with our agent's death. Wonder who he's secretly working for? He wouldn't be just a loose cannon wandering round a Greek island finding casual work.'

The policeman nodded. 'Yes I'm sure you're right.'

'I need to look in his room and see if the pneumatic gun is there?' Sarah said.

Phillip returned and squeezed her hand. He bent forward and kissed her cheek. 'I'll be as quick as I can ... promise.'

Panos tried to hide his annoyance at this sign of affection. Phillip picked up his case and followed him out onto the lane leading down to the dock. Sarah suddenly thought of the revolver in the Bible still in the wood shed. Hell, why did she leave it there? Another mistake, her mistake not Ricki's; in the drama of the evening before she had forgotten to remove the damn gun; she had to get that Bible.

9

'... the face of the devil'

The body was laid-out in a small room acting as a temporary morgue at the rear of the ferry ticket office. Panos unlocked the door and entered, switching on a single bare bulb hanging in the centre of the room. Phillip followed and took in the scene; the sparse room with cream painted walls and one blackened out window. A few hard chairs lined the walls, an olive wood trestle table with the sheet-covered body pushed hard against the far wall. Above it a large silver-framed picture of Mary and Child temporary hung to watch over the corpse. Large chunks of ice lay across most of the body making the sheet dark as it melted in the stifling heat. Phillip removed a large vase of flowers placed at the foot of the corpse. The two intruders cleared the ice away from the head. Phillip pulled back the cover to reveal the face. For a moment, he shuddered at the grotesque chalky-white features; usually in death, the face peaceful and at rest, but this mask reflecting evil he mulled. He turned the head to one side examining the smashed skull, the blood hard and dark brown. The face had several cuts and abrasions but very little blood; a sign that they had occurred after death. He paused to be thoughtful and looked at Panos. 'Could the body have moved after the fall?'

'Moved?'

'Yes. For example ... shall we say ... landed on a rock which smashed his skull, and then later, rolled further down to have caused these cuts and abrasions?'

Panos nodded. 'Sure. We had a heavy swell during the night. The sea could have lifted the body up and then dashed it further down onto other rocks. You can see the clothing is still damp with drying salt.'

Phillip felt the twisted broken neck. Both legs were broken. He pointed at the scratched hands and the dirt under the nails. Panos moved closer. 'See here, it looks as though he was grabbing at the cliff trying to stop his fall.' As Phillip picked up a corner of the sheet to cover the face, he recalled the very last line from the Greek tragedy: God of all Wars, *"he laid a cloth and hid the face of the devil"*. They recovered the corpse with the melting ice, and before leaving they both faced the body and paused for a moment giving the sign of the cross.

They breathed in the fresh seaweed-tangy air after the stifling heady atmosphere of the temporary morgue. Phillip stared out to sea thinking of the past few hours; Katie's bullet wound and the dead Romanian; the envelope he carried for the man from the Business Attaché's office ... must bring it back; whilst you're here call me Sarah not Katie; and that drowning only last week. He felt worried; those abrasions and scratches after death? He looked back at the town. He was aware that the policeman called Panos seemed anxious and watching him closely. He had to be sure so he indicated with his hand towards the cliffs. 'Where is this Santa Maria Chapel?'

Panos pointed to the western edge of the town. 'You can see the roof with the Golden Cross.'

Phillip shaded his eyes; the glinting cross unmistakable against the azure sky and seemingly floating high above the greenery of the island. 'I would like to go up there.'

The police officer hesitated and reluctantly nodded his head. 'Of course.'

Phillip felt annoyed. *Why do these people have to be so obstructive?* 'I believe you have the contents of his pockets and you also found a whisky bottle and a packet of heroin at the cliff edge?'

'Yes, his pocket contents and the bottle and heroin are in my office.'

'May I see them?'

Panos led him into his wooden hut that acted as the Port Office. He unlocked a cupboard and placed the wallet onto a wooden desk, but really it was no more than a kitchen table occupied with an ancient *Hermes* typewriter. Phillip opened the damp wallet to examine the money and one bent phone card. 'Nothing been removed from the wallet?'

Panos shrugged his shoulders. 'That's it.' He then put the empty whisky bottle and packet of heroin on the table. 'We found this with the pickup.'

'Where did he live?'

'In the wood store, behind the hotel.'

'Have you searched his room?'

'No. Give me time,' Panos replied, his voice irritated. 'I only found him about one or two hours ago. In any case, shouldn't the authorities do that?'

'Well it's hardly a crime scene,' snapped the doctor. 'It is so little for a man's life. You call him Ion. Doesn't he have a surname?'

Panos scratched his stubble and felt decidedly tired. Why can't he just sign the certificate and go away. Ion was a nobody, and nobody cares he's dead. Why Petra ever gave him work he'll never know, always snooping. The English woman was right; he must have killed that English agent. He shook his head. 'No. No surname. You would have to ask Petra for that.'

'Who's Petra?'

He rolled his eyes at the questions. 'He owns the hotel with Kelena. Ion helped him with his fishing. Petra used his boat this morning to help me look for the body.'

Phillip pulled out a notepad from his case. 'We must find his passport for his name; we need that for the certificate. I'll take these items back with me to the Examining Magistrate. I'll give you a receipt.' He finished writing and handed the paper to Panos who stared without interest at it. 'Right, would you take me up to the Chapel please?'

Panos slowly pulled alongside the chapel of Santa Maria. They opened the pickup doors and got out. As the doctor walked towards the edge Panos called out, 'just be careful. We've had many accidents here with the tourists.'

The doctor held his hand up to shade his eyes from the burning sun as he took in the paradise of the Aegean Sea. He tried to peer over and commented, 'I see what you mean having to look from the sea. Why aren't there any signs, or a fence across?'

Panos sighed, his shoulders drooping at these questions. 'We've been trying for years. I don't know what it's like on the mainland. How we'll ever manage the Olympics, should we get it, only the gods know the answer.'

Phillip examined the disturbance on the edge where the Romanian must had slipped. He murmured angrily, 'to come up here drunk *and* on drugs ... in the dark ...what a waste ... the mad fool!'

'We found the pickup where we've just parked. The driver's door was open and the radio still on. The bottle was there near the edge and the heroin next to it.' He kicked a stone over the edge, bored with the questions. 'Never did like him. There won't be any tears shed.'

Phillip stared at him. 'How dreadfully sad. Look I'm satisfied, I'll sign the certificate. Perhaps you would collect his belongings from his room and hang on to them until you hear from the Magistrate in case his family claims them. When I get back to my office I'll fill out a report and send you a copy for your files.' He looked at Panos with a slight smile. 'Do you have a filing system over here?'

Panos look bemused. 'Which answer would you like ... the official ... or the unofficial?'

Phillip smiled. 'Both.'

'When I first arrived I was told there was a system ... but then I've never found it.'

Phillip asked, 'What happens to the copy of my report when you get it?

'Put it in my office desk drawer I suppose.'

Phillip thought of the kitchen table acting as the desk in the rear of the ticket office. He thought of the organised chaos back on the mainland and suddenly seemed to relax; who is right?

'Come on Panos, let's get back to the hotel and I'll buy you a beer. I bet there's a certain young lady who is champing at the bit.'

10

'... touch her soft lips and part'

They arrived back at the hotel to find Petra still hunched over the bar staring at an empty bottle of Metaxa. There was no sign of Sarah or Kelena. Panos went behind the bar ignoring the despondent Greek and opened two beers. He picked up two glasses and they both settled outside in the shade.

They sat in silence as Phillip wrote out the death certificate until Panos called out to Petra, 'where's Kelena and the English woman?'

He shouted back from the gloom, 'they're looking at Ion's things in the wood store. She wanted me to do it but I said no ... woman's work!'

Phillip grimaced at island prejudice. The sound of voices made them turn as Kelena and Sarah came into the bar. Sarah spied the two men sitting outside and hurried through. Phillip noticed her apprehensive look as she frowned and studied his face. He half stood and pulled out a chair and she eased herself down. He called out to Kelena, 'another beer for Sarah please. Oh did you find his passport?'

The two women looked at each other and shook their heads. Kelena frowned. 'No, we packed everything of his ... but no passport.

'Well Panos, I can only put Ion on the certificate. I'll mention it in my report. That will be the Examining Magistrate's problem.'

Panos swilled his drink down. 'Thanks for the beer, I'll arrange for the ferry to take the body.' Phillip handed over the certificate and they shook hands. Panos looked at Sarah and hurried out into the lane.

She studied his face and frowned. 'Well how did you get on?'

Phillip sat quiet for a while as if reflecting on the events of the past hour and choosing his words carefully before he spoke. This seemed to concern her.

'I examined the body and have entered the cause of death as Paralysis Herniplegia; simply put, it means injury to the brain. There is the broken neck of course but I was more concerned with scratches and abrasions that must have happened after death. Somehow it didn't seem right.' He noticed her change of composure. 'However, Panos took me up to the Chapel and it was obvious that he must have slipped. It's very dangerous there and I gather that the council is extremely lapse in putting up a safety barrier, despite the number of accidents. I will mention this lapse most strongly in my report. There was dirt under his nails where he had tried to claw the edge to stop himself, so my conclusion ... a straight forward accident; bearing in mind he was drunk and on drugs it's hardly a surprise.' He watched her face regain her composure.

'Is that is what you want to hear?'

She nodded.

'I don't know, or want to know your interest in this island, but I assume it also is tied up with the so called drowning last week. I did manage to see that unofficial autopsy report at the embassy.'

She leaned forward and spoke quietly, 'Phillip, the man who you have just examined was responsible for the death of that Englishman and also responsible for creating many widows and orphans. He tried to kill me, and I would have been just another item on his list so it could have been me you examined.' She looked down at her hands. 'Please do not peel back too many layers with your report. Remember, I'm the one who has to live with my conscience and I'm only sorry you had to get involved.'

He lowered his eyes, brushed some soil from his trousers and glanced back, smiled and lifted his glass. 'I don't seem to know the young woman in front of me, but I only want to remember our childhood memories.' He offered his glass. 'Here's to you dear Katie ... to our salad days.'

She looked warmly into his eyes. 'Here's to us Phillip and those sweet memories.' They touched glasses but her sinking feeling meant this time she knew it would be his turn to run away.

Panos was as good as his word. The fast, twin-hulled, *Dolphin of the Seas* diverted to pick the doctor up in the late afternoon. Kelena had worked her magic in the kitchen and the lunch went all too quickly. They had walked arm in arm out of town through the shaded woods; Sarah feeling she was in a dream with the gentle warm breeze causing the mottled sunlight to dance through the swaying branches touched with the sweet aromatic smell of the pines; if she pinched herself she would awake and he would be gone. Once, Phillip had stopped to look up into the foliage. 'Hear that Katie?' He became engrossed by the enthralling song of a bird singing in the tree high above. 'Do you recognise it? Levantine Shearwater. I haven't heard that for years.' She recalled the hours they had spent wandering through the parks of Athens with their parents and his love of nature. She was always amazed at the way he could recognise songs from the different birds. She would never forget their walk that afternoon; the flora and its mingled scents seemed to have more beauty and perfume than ever, the singularity of the view across the blue sea most magical; the tiny dots of white sails scattered across the horizon and the distant mauve islands floating in a ghostly cushion of distorted heat haze; beckoning, adding to the moment she wanted to last forever. She knew she would never again experience his closeness; soon he would be gone and she knew Athina would never again allow their paths to cross.

The eventual walk to the jetty, her arm tightly gripping his, dreading what she knew would be their final parting ... and this was it ... that sinking feeling tightened as the *Dolphin of the Seas* reversed out, rapidly turned, and headed back towards the mainland. Phillip gave a last wave with his hat before disappearing inside.

Panos had been watching them earlier; he had wondered as she flung her arms around her friend and he had to gently push her away; the doctor putting his hand under her chin, lifting her face up to look at him as he seemed to speak firmly to her; she had nodded and stood back wiping her eyes, now she remained standing at the far end of the quay, her hands shading her eyes from the sinking sun until her visitor from the past merged into the haze. She turned and slowly wandered past, staring down at the ground with her regrets on another time past; he pretended not to notice by studying his clipboard.

She paused and glanced back once more to the sea wanting him to suddenly be there; hoping Phillip hadn't really gone, but he had. As she approached the hotel, her dispirited features changed and she straightened, quickening her step. She asked Kelena for a coffee and sat on the terrace, trying to concentrate on the evening ahead.

Kelena brought two coffees and sat down looking at her face; she understood. She put her hand on Sarah's. 'Do you mind Sarah or would you rather be on your own?'

Sarah shook her head and put her hand on Kelena's arm. 'No of course not!'

'He seems to be good ... your friend, even though he is a Greek man.'

'Yes he is a lovely man,' she murmured wistfully. 'There are good and bad from all countries. You have only experienced Petra. Was he born here?'

'Yes!' She twisted her finger into her brow and snorted. 'Island mentality; they think this island is the Corinthian centre of the world. I was born in Athens and that's where I should have stayed.' Her dark eyes glaring through her rimmed glasses.

'How did you and Petra meet?'

'I came here when I was seventeen. My parents brought me for a holiday. It is strange because when the ferry started to dock I had a bad feeling and told my mother I didn't want to stay. I wanted to turn back. I got vibes from the island. My mother had seemed apprehensive on the trip over, which wasn't like her. I remember my father being very quiet and wandering around the ferry. Of course it wasn't anything like it is today. The ferry was slow and not a car ferry; everything had to be off-loaded by crane. Well of course there weren't any cars on the island, only donkeys and bicycles. Guess which family had the only island telephone?'

Sarah couldn't help smiling.

'We stayed at their hotel near the other end of the beach.' She indicated with her head and Sarah could just make out the tall red-coloured roof appearing above two new houses. 'Petra was their son. I was introduced to him and he seemed amusing at the time; a bit older than me. I was young and naive. What I did not understand was that this was an arranged marriage and they were the dominate family here, so I was told that Petra was a good catch. His family seemed to run the island.' She looked thoughtful. 'This showed by the fact they didn't have donkeys they owned two mules.'

Sarah bit her lip and turned her face away. 'How long ago was this?'

She hesitated and twisted her wedding ring 'Twenty-two years!'

'And you agreed?'

'Yes. You must understand I was getting away from my parents. As a young girl, I could not do anything without a chaperon. They completely controlled my life.' She raised her hands to the sky. 'At last I was going to be free. The idea was wonderful. I thought that this must be love so I embraced it. How would I know any different?' She held her hands to her chest and looked towards her shrine. 'In my childish naivety I assumed that this was what she wanted for me.' She gave the sign of the cross.

The conversation went quiet as the man, to whom she described as amusing, slouched through nodding to Sarah, a squid in one hand, a string of red snapper in the other and they heard the thud as he threw them on the kitchen table. He opened the back door and slammed it shut heading for the wood store. Kelena glanced at Sarah. 'See what I mean. I do not exist; in fact, women here do not exist; only for work. He only acknowledged you because,' she rubbed two fingers together; 'you pay money.'

'So you became engaged? When did that happen?'

'At the end of our so called holiday; our marriage was announced and arrangements were made for my mother and I to return two weeks later for one night.'

'But why one night?' Sarah raised her cup and drank.

Kelena laughed and shook her head. 'Sarah you do not understand our ways. No, let me correct myself, not modern Greece ways. Not mainland ways ... *Island ways*. We came back for one night so he could sleep with me...'

Sarah spluttered her coffee and put the cup back on the table, wiping her mouth with a tissue. She couldn't think of anything to say but sat staring at the woman with both her eyebrows raised.

'If he didn't like me then the marriage would have been called off and shame brought on my mother for not bringing me up correct.'

Sarah ran her hand through her hair and grimaced. 'This is medieval,' she exclaimed. 'I had no idea this still went on. Why shame on your mother?

'Family honour I suppose.'

'What would happen if you didn't like him?'

'The woman's feeling doesn't come into it,' she spat out. 'She is nothing.'

'Have you ever considered divorce?'

She threw her head back and laughed. 'Then it comes back to family honour and shame on my family.' She rose and stood in front of her shrine. She made the sign of the cross. 'This is what she ordained for me and I must follow her path. What I need is a miracle.' She turned back to Sarah taking in her intense eyes. 'Maybe she sent you to help; a free spirit. Follow your heart Sarah.'

Sarah mused. 'Good advice Kelena, I certainly will.'

'Now I must prepare the fish for tonight's meal. As you had a large lunch will you want dinner tonight?'

Sarah shook her head. 'No. I think I'll skip dinner tonight thank you. I'll go for a walk instead.'

'Then that is three meals less. Mr. Podolski and Danni say they are dining with friends.' She smiled. 'I can't imagine Mr. Podolski having friends ... but then he is a guest and I shouldn't say that, should I?' Her eyes twinkled and she disappeared into the kitchen.

'... gathering clouds'

There had been fair-weather cumulous clouds gathering during the late afternoon, suggesting possible thunderstorms that evening. So Sarah packed her waterproof cape on top of the Uher sat-recorder and slipped the back pack across her shoulders. This caused her to winch as the dressing pulled. She swallowed some pain killers, checked the berretta and adjusted her shoulder holster. She looked at the dead Romanian's desecrated bible on her bed; its uncomfortable truth concealed from prying eyes. She managed to hide it from Kelena when earlier they searched the wood store. She sealed it in a plastic bag and pushed the package behind a tub of green foliage on the balcony. Dressed in a dark top and shorts, she pulled on her trainers and slipped out the back of the hotel. The murky light from the cloud cover helped to mask her movement as she reached the road leading out of town. The Beachcomber had just started coming to life with the distinctive voice of Nana Mouskouri and the holiday punters adding their lamentable wailing to *The White Rose of Athens*. She stood behind a wall trying to ignore the music but finding she was mouthing the words into the evening air as the old Escort appeared over the hill to stop in the shadow just beyond the wall. She opened the door, putting her pack in first and carefully sitting, sensitive to her wound.

Ricki looked at her. 'Hi. How is it?'

She nodded. 'OK.'

He leaned towards her. 'As you're my date for the evening do I get a kiss?' he asked.

'You're pushing your luck. You might need those snow boots if you don't behave yourself.'

He laughed and swung the car round, heading back up the hill. The dying sun rays broke through the gathering clouds, adding a pink surrealism of surprise across the distant islands. The extraordinary beauty jolted her memory of Phillip waving his painful goodbye. At that moment she felt lonely, the last person on the planet, wishing she was a thousand miles away ... anywhere but driving along a bumpy, dusty road on an island in Greece. Ricki paused at the Chapel for a moment, no words spoken, just thoughts and carried on.

The car lights were turned off before crawling along the dusky track where Sarah had ridden her moped. Ricki parked the car behind a bush and through the fading light they could see the wooden bridge leading to the small island. Sarah lifted up her backpack pulling out the Uher sat-recorder and placing it on her lap.

Ricki looked at the machine. 'What is this supposed to do then?'

'I told you before. Why don't you listen?'

He quickly changed the subject. 'How did you get on with the doctor? Did he ask too many questions?'

She shook her head and told him the events of the day. He whistled through his teeth and chuckled. 'So he bought it then, hook, line and sinker.'

He suddenly saw her eyes flash in the half-light. 'No, he didn't buy anything,' she snapped back.

Her outburst surprised him.

'He knew exactly what happened.' Her eyes were moist. 'I don't want you talking about him like that.'

He had touched a nerve. 'I'm sorry I didn't mean anything. Good job he was from the embassy I guess.'

She turned her face away, tears running down her cheeks. He didn't like to see her cry; *I must be getting soft,* he thought. He opened his door. 'I'll go and check around whilst you get the receiver going.' She nodded and he pulled himself out. He wandered over to the edge of the drop, staring across the water to the island he had just left. He glanced back. *Wonder who this embassy doctor is? Something has happened to upset her.* He looked at his watch. 'Guess the visitors should be arriving soon.' He could see her bent over the receiver, so he went back and she wound the window down.

'It's working great ... listen.'

He leaned closer and heard the voice of Henry asking what wine should he open? Johnnie's heavy voice shouted across the room: 'Don't get the good stuff, they're Romanians, they wouldn't know the difference between champagne and cat's pee.' The voices mechanical and tinny.

Sarah looked at Ricki and pulled a face. 'What an ignoramus moron you've had to live with!'

He looked surprised at her observation. 'Now you can see what I've had to put up with on this island paradise.'

She looked thoughtful and commented, 'paradise can also mean, *"the abode of the righteous dead awaiting Judgment Day".*'

'Well I wouldn't know about that, would I?'

She noticed the trace of sarcasm. She handed him the recorder through the window and she got out, leaning back in to grab her night-glasses from her pack.

He studied the recorder. 'Did they show you how to use this thing?' And by the look on her face he wished he hadn't asked.

She ignored his remark and asked, 'where did you stick the bug?'

'On the lounge sliding door. It also covers the dining area, and even the terrace, not that they'll sit out there. Somehow the mosquitoes seem to like Johnny.'

She observed. 'Well I'm glad something does.'

Johnnie's voice sounded nearer: 'Glad we got rid of that Ricki, didn't think he was going. He's got a girl in town; she'll keep him occupied for a few hours.'

She stared at him.

'Did you see him go, Henry?' Silence. Johnnie shouted: 'I'm

talking to you Henry. Did you see him drive off?'

'Yes.'

'Glad when this is over. Don't trust this Polski ... or whatever his name is ... shifty looking bastard!'

Henry's voice, correcting: 'Podolski.'

'Right ... Podolski! We've gotta be on our guard, and don't open your mouth and put your foot in it. We're going to keep our cards close to our chest. OK?'

They both imagined Henry nodding. Sarah pressed the red button. 'I think we should start recording all this.'

Johnnie's voice, '... and another thing, keep your mouth tight about that drowning. It was you that blurted out about him coming and we suddenly get London hot footing it down here with that blasted woman poking her nose.'

She noticed Ricki's grin and stared back at the recorder.

'... we can make a load of bees and honey on this deal.'

Ricki whispered, 'He means money.'

'I'm not stupid,' she snapped back.

An unexpected sharp noise from the recorder made them jump.

Ricki muttered 'that must be the sliding door closing. Hope the bug hasn't dropped off.'

Johnnie's voice. 'Petromos is the perfect stepping stone to the mainland. That blasted creep Ion, gets drunk and falls over the cliff. He had that fishing boat all geared up to collect the delivery, so we've now got another problem to solve. That Petra was beginning to get suspicious as to why that Ion wanted his boat and I suppose he would've been brought in with a share, or dealt with.'

Henry. 'How about this Panos then? He's involved with London so I don't think we can trust him.'

'Don't worry about him. He'll take a bung.'

Sarah glanced at her companion.

He nodded back. 'Bribe.'

She huffed. 'Why can't you Londoners' speak English?'

He whispered, 'It started when they were trading illegally so the cops wouldn't understand.'

She pulled a face. 'OK, I didn't ask for a history lesson,' glaring back at the recorder.

He straightened. *Oh dear, she's decidedly missing her doctor;* he felt a sudden desire to put his arm around her as the sound of a car passed behind, its tyres crunching on its way down to the jetty.

The headlights of the taxi swung round, the sensor switching on the floodlighting and illuminating the colourful bobbing boats; the illuminated taxi-light casting an orange glow over the features of the man getting out from the front passenger seat. Sarah recognised Danni through her night binoculars hurrying to open the rear door and helping a slow moving figure. For a moment, the orange light shone on the cruel face of Shumonko Podolski. Her glasses focused into his cold, white soulless eye-sockets and for one moment he seemed to stare straight back into hers, as if he knew she was there, bringing an icy wave up her back; she let out an involuntary shiver that made Ricki lower his glasses to glance at his companion. The dog started to bark and the shadowy figure of Henry appeared, shutting the kennel door and unlocking the gate.

The taxi reversed and shot forward up the road, its engine echoing through the sleeping trees, its lights stabbing the road as it passed behind them; they were left with the sudden quietness and the chirping sounds of crickets that only night brings; Johnnie's voice occasionally breaking the silence. Sarah turned the volume down to a whisper. A security light came on from the island and they watched as the jetty floodlight switched off and the two men walked hesitantly across the wooden bridge, the young man supporting Shumonko Podolski into the darkness beyond the light. After a short pause the light vanished, leaving the area in blackness. On the horizon a sudden ominous flash of lightning; the recorder crackled.

The two eavesdroppers listening to the curious tinny noises of doors opening and clicking shut. Johnnie's voice dominating the recording, welcoming his guests, glasses clinking and then a few moments silence as they settled down.

She recognised the pinched, whiney voice of Podolski re-starting the conversation with a high husky cough: 'Are these your paintings?' he demanded.

Johnnie's voice. 'Sure. What do you think?'

'Not to my taste.'

The two listeners chuckled. More silence until Johnnie's voice broke out: 'OK Podolski, we might as well get down to business. You've got certain items and you need help to get them into the UK?'

'That is correct. I understand that you still have contacts there, despite your history with various groups in the UK who would be very interested in finding your exact location? Old scores I think you call it?'

'Sure. We have a slight problem now because your Ion decides to get drunk and fall off a cliff. Personally I'm delighted to see the back of him. Creepy sod. Because of him we have London crawling all over us. Why the hell did he have to shoot that man? What did that prove?'

Sarah murmured, 'so he did know about the shooting.'

'More than I did,' complained Ricki.

Podolski whined. 'Yes I agree, that was a stupid mistake. But London will go away. I have contacts there that will snuff out any further investigation.'

She glanced with a worried look at Ricki and whispered, 'what does he mean, by contacts? Janus will be concerned.'

Johnnie's voice sounded hesitant and growled, 'that officer from London suggested that I might be pulled out from here because of the killing … for my own safety!'

'You don't have to worry about your safety even if they remove your protection. Stay here, I can look after you. I can arrange for my London contact to get rid of him. The last thing we want is to have the law sitting on your doorstep. I'll get him away and you will take your chances. Where is your London bobby tonight?'

The two listeners glanced at each other and they heard him give a high pitched womanly laugh. 'I'm surprised he doesn't have one of those absurd tall hats or is that just for the tourists?'

''ere, don't you start that Podolski; they're my bobbies you're talking about. There's nothing wrong with a London bobby ... that a few back-handers can't fix.' He roared with laughter. ''Ain't that right, Henry?'

'Sure! That's right boss.'

'I asked you ... where is he tonight?' whined Podolski.

'He's out with his girlfriend, getting sloshed down at the Beachcomber I wouldn't wonder.'

'Sloshed?'

They didn't hear his answer as there was a call from Henry that dinner was ready. Ricki leaned over and whispered in her ear, 'so we're getting sloshed are we?'

She pushed him, moving her head away, trying to listen above the scraping chairs.

Podolski's voice. 'Where is this officer from London now?'

'Probably returned to London. We haven't seen her since the other day.'

'Her. You mean a woman? What are they doing sending a woman?' His voice more icy and sharp.

The conversation becoming difficult to hear over the clatter of the cutlery so they leaned towards the Uher, straining to hear so Sarah turned the volume up. The evening was drawing in, the ominous cloud cover becoming heavy, a sudden distant roll of thunder; the recording distorted with static; the bluish glow from the recorder casting an eerie icy light across their faces.

They heard Podolski's high pitched nasal voice. 'What does this woman look like ... this agent from London?'

'Hell!' Sarah pulled a face.

Johnnie: 'A woman! What more can I say. About thirty.'

Sarah's companion leaned over and whispered, 'I would have said younger myself.'

At last he noticed her first smile of the evening.

Podolski's nasal voice again. 'Blondish? Once you've seen one you've seen them all.'

Johnnie. 'You wouldn't think she could hurt a fly but you should have seen what she did to our so called bodyguard.' They heard him snigger. 'Garden lizard she called him.' He laughed again.

Ricki tried to ignore her glance and the slight twitch at the corners of her mouth.

' 'ad him on the ground! He tried to creep up behind her but ...' He must have slapped the table as it made them jump, 'she had him pinned down. I loved it.' He laughed. 'Not so arrogant now.'

She held her hand to her mouth to suppress her snigger, her shoulders started to shake.

'Yeah, yeah, very funny,' Ricki growled, 'I won't live that down. And what's this about a garden lizard?'

She wiped her eyes with a tissue. 'Sorry Ricki.'

He put a hand on her shoulder. 'Well at least it cheered you up.'

She returned the gesture by putting her hand on his, leaving it there for a moment, pulling it away as another voice, probably the young man Danni, piped up. 'Sounds like that young woman staying at our hotel. She's on her own. She seems very friendly with the owner's wife and always on the telephone.'

'Well Danni, you'll have to deal with her now that Romanian bastard is dead.' Podolski's voice cut a chilling edge. 'We can't let some peasant woman get in our way. What's her name?'

'I think they call her Sarah.'

She glanced at Ricki, her face seething with anger. 'Damn him!'

She felt his hand grip her shoulder. 'You can't stay there Sarah,' his voice worried, 'we've got to get you away.'

'Don't think about it, let's concentrate on tonight.'

The evening wore on with more information starting to unravel. Drugs and guns were the shipment and the first consignment arranged for the evening after next. It was Ion who was going to steal Petra's boat and meet a cargo ship at midnight, bring the delivery into the small jetty and put the cargo into a waste skip before the return of the other fishing boats. The skip would be picked up the following morning, and then shipped over to Piraeus on the ferry. From there onto a lorry bound for northern

France and then the UK; the cargo load being split into four bundles in the event any one route was infiltrated and broken; Greece - Sardinia - Spain - Portugal.

Johnnie's voice broke in, 'what we going to do with getting the boat now this bastard Ion's gone? How 'bout this Petra, the one whose boat it is. Wouldn't he play ball; the idea of sausage and mash in his hand?'

There was silence and Sarah's companion sniggered.

Then Podolski's whine. 'What is this you say ... sausage and what?'

'I thought your English was good Podolski. Tell him Henry, teach our friend real English ... London English.'

'Sausage and mash,' came Henry's voice. 'Cash ... cash in the hand.'

'Your language is hard enough without this sausage and mash. Yes good idea. He seems like the type that wouldn't say no ... to sausage and mash,' agreed Podolski.

They thought they heard Henry's laugh.

Sarah shook her head and pressed the stop button. 'I think we have enough info for London.' The talk had turned, becoming inane chatter and laughter as the drink changed over to whisky; Johnnie was now inebriated and his words slurred; Podolski with his high-pitched whine most piercing and tinny through the *Uher*; Sarah picturing his cruel eyes with disgust. She glanced at Ricki. 'Hope they have a cockney interpreter in London ... wonder what Janus will make of it? Here comes the clever bit.'

She took a black flat pack from her bag and opened the lid revealing a tiny keyboard. She handed the recorder to Ricki who nearly dropped it. 'Careful,' she reacted sharply. 'Hedge Farm would go berserk if I took it back broken. I had to sign for it.'

He whispered back, 'sorry, I must be nervous. The last time we were this close; you had me on the ground ... remember?'

She nodded; her eyes gleamed in the moonlight. 'Yes. That was sweet. I won't let you forget it.'

'I suppose you can't wait to get back and let London have a laugh.'

'How did you guess,' was her reply.

She typed a message to Janus, and then plugged a cable from the pack into the Uher. She felt him leaning closer, they stared as a narrow red strip-light appeared; twisting the pack until the red flickered and changed to amber locking onto the satellite. He looked up to the heaven. 'Nice to know she's still on duty.'

Sarah glanced at him. 'Ready?' He nodded. She looked at her watch and pressed the send button, counting. The amber flickered green - sent – *info detail* – *date* – then faded.

They looked at each other. 'Five seconds for all that length of recording,' she whispered, 'and it's now sitting in Janus's hard-drive ... we hope.' She raised her eyebrows and murmured, 'amazing!' Suddenly *message received* flashed, the screen faded and she closed the lid.

She looked upward. 'Can you hear it?'

His face was curious and he cocked his ear. 'Hear what, the satellite?'

'No ... listen. That bird singing?'

'Ah yes. Wonder what it is? I often hear it.'

'It's a Levantine Shearwater,' she commented warmly, 'I heard one this afternoon.'

'Gosh, I'm impressed, ma'am.'

A flash lit the heavy sky and one second later they both jumped at the crack of thunder; the promised rain starting with heavy drops splashing down from the tight overhead foliage, drenching and pounding the desperately dry ground, then a tinny drumming from the Escort. Ricki shouted above the downpour as they hurried to the car, 'it's the satellite saying, *"message sent and goodnight."'*

She paused a moment, staring up to the heavens, rain running down her face, whispering, 'no, it's always Athina.'

'... and now the hungry lion roars'

The muddy Escort pulled in behind the hotel, the wipers protesting, squeaking against the glass, fighting the heavy rain all the way back and reminding them of Podolski's irritating voice; she amused herself, *mister-squeaky-creepy*. The colourful flashing lights from Beachcomber danced across the puddled waste ground, raucous laughter and screams above the music jolting her senses back into the noisy world of holiday island fantasy. They watched the punters jammed inside the tavern escaping the sudden downpour, adding to their fun.

They hadn't spoken on the journey back, but Ricki suddenly asked, 'what are we going to do ma'am, now Podolski seems to be on to you?'

She dragged her thoughts back. 'They won't try anything tonight, they'll be too drunk. We'll think clearer in the morning. The talk of bribing Petra might play into our hands.'

He thought he could see a hint of a smile. She nodded. 'I have an idea ... actually I might be able to kill two birds with one stone; and don't tell me that's a cockney expression.'

'No we would say ...'

She put her hand across his mouth. 'I've had enough cockney talk for one night.'

'OK, another night then,' he muttered through her hand.

'Be interesting to know how Janus reacts after listening to the recording; and what he'll do? Especially Podolski saying contacts; don't like the sound of *contacts*.' Sarah continued, moving her hand away from his mouth.

He agreed and nodded. 'That's how they knew our agent was coming and Ion blew it. Had his own agenda I guess. But then of course, you wouldn't be sitting in the rain with me. Could have been me of course,' he added thoughtfully. He looked at her. 'What would a certain Miss Sarah Athina-Beaumont have been doing in London this evening if she hadn't been sitting in the rain with a garden lizard?'

She grinned. 'Ironing probably ... how about you?'

'Probably playing snooker with the boys.'

'Thought you would have been with one of the girlfriends,' she suggested, pointedly.

'They don't seem to last. Maybe I'm too fussy.'

She laughed. 'Or too arrogant, as I heard tonight ... maybe they're too fussy.' She noticed he didn't respond. She shivered and rubbed her arms. 'I'm going in now. I'm getting cold sitting here. At least this evening has been positive and I'm sure it'll have London running round in circles. I can imagine the flap in the morning when Janus gets in.'

She opened the door and swung her legs round, sitting for a while before pulling herself out. She grimaced and held her side. She leaned back in and smiled. 'Well done *agent* Ricki. Ten out of ten I think tonight.'

'Yes ma'am, I agree. As apparently you're my date tonight, do I get a goodnight kiss?'

She resisted an impulse to say yes, but only added, 'as you Londoners say ... on your bike mate.'

He grinned and turned the car round, winding his window down shouting above the rain and the intrusive Beachcomber, 'I'll wait in the woods until Podolski and his mate clear off ... and as you say in the shires ... tally-ho old girl.' The Escort shot off, splashing through a large puddle.

Keeping her head dry with the backpack above her head from the heavy rain, she waited until the Escort's lights passed from view over the hill. Pulling the Velcro strap apart loosening the covert-fit holster to ease the ache in her side, she headed back to her room; from now on she knew she would have to be extra vigilant.

She checked the unbroken strand of hair across the bedroom door jamb before entering and bolting the door. Stripping off her wet clothing she eased away the wound dressing; it still looked red and tender but no apparent infection. She suddenly shivered again, the sudden heavy rain causing the temperature to plummet, but the hot shower that cascaded down over her aching body was delicious and agreeable, bringing a wave of weariness to her limbs with the thought of bed so desirable. She dried and redressed the wound the way Phillip had shown her. *Gosh was that only today?* Phillip had now gone, and she was on her own with an injury, and a man called Podolski who had threatened to harm her. She took her painkillers and sank into bed. For the first hour she slept the so called sleep of kings, but the image and sound of windscreen wipers squeaking and scraping back and forward caused her to turn and twist in her sleep. Gradually she awoke to the sonorous hissing of heavy rain hitting the shrubbery outside her balcony; the constant drip-drip of one of Petra's leaking gutters brought her fully awake.

She then became aware of groaning voices and noises from the corridor outside her room. It went quiet but suddenly she heard her door handle twist. She grabbed the Beretta from under her pillow and swung her feet to the ground; her heart pounding. She stared at the corridor light streaming from under her door. Then she could hear another handle being tried to the room next door; a German voice, deep and angry, responding from being awoken, shouting, 'Verschwinden Sie!'

She held her breath at the whispering and unsteady feet shuffling and scuffing up the tiled steps leading to the floor above; the corridor light clicked off, back into darkness, and she took a deep breath, her adrenalin still racing. Above, a door slammed with scraping of furniture on the tiled floor; more mumbling and groaning. She thought she recognised the high whine of Podolski; the sharp snap of a light switch sounding through her ceiling, and then silence. Turning on her bed light she looked at her watch ... half-past-one … *is that all?* She sighed and lay back, feeling her adrenalin still pumping. *What the hell was all that about?* The downpour still persisted and she stared at the blank ceiling, mulling over events in her troubled mind. She assessed her next step. I *must involve Panos. He's very friendly with Petra, and maybe, with a bit of manipulation, he'll persuade him into taking the bribe and collect the cargo tomorrow night … and then Petra will be putty in my hand.*

Sarah suddenly relaxed because it all seemed to be coming together; she smiled and turned off the light.

Awaking strangely refreshed, her side didn't ache so much and things seemed clearer in her mind. Apart from the threat from Podolski she knew what to do. Janus would ring as soon as he'd heard the recording. She looked at her watch, six thirty. She yawned and stretched. 'Must get up … go and see Panos before breakfast.'

She climbed the short flight of steps leading up the side of the white-washed Spiti and rang the bell. Anchored half a mile outside the jetty reach, a water barge waited with its cargo of fresh water to come in for its twice weekly discharge. The port side was deserted; normal people would be in bed of course. The overnight rain had cleared, the air delightfully fresh, the warm early morning sun streaked across the concrete, already drying the puddles. The deep blue of the sea in contrast to the translucent sky, common gulls swooping and picking at the debris left over from the fish cargo carried from Ingissi the morning before. She thought she saw a pair of Shrikes swooping, competing against the gulls; Phillip would be impressed with her recognition of the birds.

She rang the bell again. 'Come on Panos.' Despite her dark glasses, she squinted, trying to shade her eyes from the dazzling glare coming off the Spiti's white wall. Sounds of a key turning, the thick wooden blue painted door opened slightly. Panos squinted through the gap, blinking in the early sun. His eyes were heavy and blurred and he peered carefully at his visitor until they focused. Suddenly his face broke into recognition and he opened the door a fraction more. 'Oh it's you,' he croaked. He coughed to clear his throat. 'Sorry but I had a heavy night. What can I do for you?'

'At first you can let me in. We need to talk.'

He hesitated but resigned himself. 'Come on in ... but I'm not dressed for visitors.' He opened the door wider and she followed him in. He was dressed only in jogging pants, his hair wild and his chin with a heavy growth of stubble. He scratched his head yawning. 'I won't be a minute, I'll get a shirt ... must put the kettle on ... fancy a coffee?' he mumbled and disappeared out of the room.

'Yes please ... black and no sugar. Bet you were at the Beachcomber bar?' she shouted.

His croaky voice came back through the doorway, 'how'd you guess? I got into bed about two this morning.'

She took in the room and was pleasantly surprised; it being agreeably tidy, the early morning orange sun cutting through the window making the white-painted rustic room light and welcoming. A heavy double planked dining table with chairs, sat under the window and a two-seater settee, covered with a highly coloured cotton sheet thrown across, faced a large television in the corner. Next to the television, a compact disc unit together with a tall CD rack. Hanging from one wall were several old and faded sepia photographs; family groups and one caught her eye, a distinguished looking white haired man in a suit, together with a middle aged woman standing behind a young boy and girl. She immediately recognised Panos as the child, his features taking after his mother. She became aware of one item missing from the room, there were no religious icons.

Dominating the room on the far wall stood a set of shelves laden with old leather books of all sizes. Interested she moved across and studied the familiar titles, *Homer's Iliad – Plato's Apology – Dinarchus Against Aristogiton*; dozens more on Greek history; few titles she didn't know; they took her back again to university and her studies. She ran her hand across the musty-smelling spines, sensing the age and legends contained in the volumes. Suddenly she was aware of Panos behind her with two mugs of coffee. He had untangled and combed his hair, his jogging-top mottled dark with water he had splashed over his face to waken himself up.

She sat on the settee and he perched opposite on a dining chair. They both sipped their coffee until he suddenly smiled at her.

But she spoke first, 'sorry to drag you from your bed.' She looked across at the books. 'I'm impressed Panos ... I studied Greek classics for my degree at Oxford but I didn't realise you were a man of classics?'

He glanced across at the books, laughed and shrugged his shoulders. 'They're not mine. I inherited them from my father. He was Professoro of Greek Classics at Ilissia University. That's where I was brought up.'

Her face lit up. 'And I was brought up just off Periandron Avenue. I went to the English school near the University.'

He looked surprised. 'You lived there as a child?'

She nodded. 'Until I was twelve. My brother and I were born at the hospital. My father was the Ambassador's secretary.'

'So do you speak Greek?'

Sarah nodded. 'Yes, but I would rather you kept that to yourself. I don't know why I'm telling you all this.'

He put his mug down and spread his hands. He continued in Greek. 'I am very impressed. Thank you for telling me. Ah ... your old friend, the doctor, is he from your childhood?'

She nodded. 'Panos ... first I must tell you about last night ...'

He listened carefully, his face serious and sober; she then explained why she needed him to talk to Petra.

'So, do I tell him he will be approached by this Danni?'

'Yes. There's no need to tell him what it's about because you shouldn't know. All he needs to know is he'll be approached to take his boat out tomorrow night. He's not to ask any questions and he must be surprised when he's asked. Tell him they'll probably pay him good money, and tell him to keep his mouth shut.'

'If he thinks there's money involved, he'll do it. He's used to keeping his trap shut. It wouldn't be the first time I've turned a blind eye to his activates ... many times in fact. This man who threatens you, what are you going to do, you can't stay at the hotel?'

'I don't know but this should be over soon.'

He gestured. 'You can stay here ... he wouldn't know you are here.'

She laughed. 'In your Spiti ... Come on!'

He frowned, obviously hurt. 'Please Miss Sarah, I am serious. I have two bedrooms here. I know I have a reputation but it's all an act. I respect you and I can't risk my money from London.' He grinned and rolled his eyes to the ceiling. 'I've seen what you can do to a man.'

'Thank you, it may come to that.' She looked at her watch. 'I must get back to the hotel. I'm expecting a reaction from London this morning.'

He looked at the clock on the far wall. 'Yes and I better get dressed. I want that water barge discharged and away before the early ferry docks.'

She stood and moved to the door, as she opened it to the bright sunlight she looked back. 'And who is the young lady in that picture on the window sill?'

His face crumbled as he stared at the photo. 'My wife,' he murmured, picking up and kissing the picture.

'What happened?'

He hesitated and spoke bitterly, 'she ran off with an English holiday maker.'

The sides of her mouth twitched and she tried to contain a smile. 'Sorry I asked ... must go.' Before she closed the door she glanced back at the sad figure clutching his framed picture and thought of Phillip sailing away from her for good. *No it isn't funny, it hurts.*

The deserted port; still empty with just the high screeching of gulls, squabbling and diving into the shimmering sea. Outside the reach, the waiting water barge gently rising and dropping in the early morning swell.

'... *doth protest too much*'

Kelena greeted her on the terrace. 'Have you been for a walk?'

'Yes, it is such a lovely morning so I thought I'd stroll around the port.'

She looked at her watch. 'You had a telephone call from your Uncle Alec about half an hour past. He said he would call a little later. Come and sit down and I'll get your breakfast ... but first a coffee.' She moved into the bar and Sarah looked around; she was the first one in and doubted if Podolski would be down for a while.

Kelena called through from the bar, 'did you hear the rain last night? I had difficulty in sleeping but it cooled the air, thank God.'

'Someone came in about half past one this morning. Sounded if they had too much to drink.'

Kelena put a jug of coffee on the table. She lowered her voice, 'Yes, I was just packing up. It was mister Podolski and the young man Danni. Danni seemed OK but the other was in a bad way. Apparently they went out to friends for the evening.' She shook her head. 'I can't imagine him having friends. I must ask Ivan the taxi driver where they went?'

'Ivan ...? That's not a Greek name.'

'No. He's east European. He came here about two years ago and took over the island taxi.' Her voice sharpened. 'Why Christos ever sold is a mystery? His family had the taxi for years. Now he spends his days in the Beachcomber bar. Rumour is he's blown the money.' Her eyes glared with anger. 'Mental ... all of them. We're gradually losing our identity.'

The telephone rang and Kelena nodded. 'That'll be your Uncle Alec. Perhaps you should take it.'

Sarah took her coffee into the reception as Kelena grinned and called after her, 'this uncle ... young is he?'

'I wish,' she called back.

She placed the battery next to the phone and pressed the + terminal and a red light flickered. She picked up the receiver and the faint humming of the scramble audible. 'Good morning uncle.'

'Good morning Katie. Well, that's an interesting postcard I received last night—'

Sarah interrupted. 'I have to admit I still have difficulty taking in this modern technology; five seconds it took to post, and it didn't even need a stamp.'

Janus laughed. 'I'm older than you and I still find the telephone amazing. I think the boffins will be impressed. Katie we have to move fast. First of all I'm concerned for your safety, these bastards are vicious. We've already lost one agent.'

'Don't worry about me. I'm more concerned about his remark, '*contact in London*'. What does he mean?'

'Yes. I have to look into that ... very worrying. I'm the only one here who knows about the recording and that's the way I'm keeping it. As far as the office is concerned I'm putting it about that we've lost interest in your Greek island, and I am pulling you and Ricki out, as well as abandoning Johnnie to his fate. Be interesting if that information gets back to Johnnie. If it does then we know we have a security problem. Johnnie will protest too much me thinks.'

There was a pause as she heard him rustling through some papers.

Janus continued. 'I've already been in touch with those other countries mentioned, and the consensus is to let it all go ahead and let the consignments arrive in the UK, then do one swoop all the way down the line. I've also let Interpol know where this Podolski is ... and interestingly, I was eventually put through to the French DGSE and spoke to a Capitainé Andre Herisson.

He was very interested in Podolski, but was a little reticent and seemed to want me to keep away from him for now. I have the impression we're treading on each other's toes. However we shall have to see, and for the moment nobody goes near him ... yet. How about this Petra character? Can you get him to play ball?'

'That's already taken care of, that's why I wasn't in earlier.'

'Ah. Well done. You must reassure him he won't be in trouble. He might be a useful contact later on. Oh, I meant to ask, how's your side?'

'Very good thank you!'

' ... and the doctor, OK?'

'Yes ...' she hesitated. 'Actually he's lovely, but I'll tell you about him later on.'

'Oh dear, I'm jealous. Look I'll be back later, but for goodness sake keep a low profile and stick within the town.'

The phone went dead and she pressed the - terminal as the door opened and Geraldine entered, followed by husband Harold.

'Good morning dear, we've missed you. Have you been having a super time? We went island-hopping to Agrissos yesterday. Spent the morning in the market and shopping in the afternoon, didn't us dear?'

Harold nodded and closed his eyes.

'Didn't see you last night for supper? Kelena said you had lunch, with a *gentleman* friend.' She raised an eyebrow waiting for Sarah's reply which didn't come. She continued, 'in fact there was hardly anyone in last night. Felt as if we had been deserted.' She shrugged and whispered, 'even *mister creepy* ... such a strange gentleman ... and his companion abandoned us.'

Kelena came in with Sarah's breakfast and the couple went to sit down at their table. Geraldine continued, 'Kelena, I've been meaning to ask you, we went for a walk the other day,' she indicated with her arm, 'right up there on the headland. We came across the most hideous dump with the rubbish tipped over the cliff edge. It was frightful. All those flies and the smell! I said to Harold, what is going on here? This is supposed to be a holiday island … it shouldn't be allowed.'

Harold piped up, 'I thought all the rubbish was taken daily to the mainland in those yellow containers?'

They all turned as the deep drone of the ferry's siren echoed across the bay; Kelena instantly glanced at her watch as she had done every day over all those years. She nodded. 'I despair of that rubbish. Yes it is terrible, and sometimes, if the wind blows from the south we can smell it, even here.'

'Why is it there?'

'That's where it used to be burnt, but them in Athens say no,' she wagged her finger, 'no more! The EEC says no more can you burn because of the environment.' She scratched her head. 'So it is left there until they make up their minds what to do. Six months it lay until they start bringing those yellow containers over every day in the summer and twice a week in the winter. But the old rubbish, it stays there, forever. The rats love it of course so what good does that do for the environment I have to ask myself? From the boat you see the scar down the cliff.' She glared and shook her head before disappearing into the kitchen.

'Such a pity,' commented Geraldine, 'such a pity.'

They looked up as Petra hurried through; grunting with what they assumed was a greeting. He carried more red snappers and disappeared into the kitchen. Just then the telephone rang in the reception and Sarah called out, 'it might be for me Kelena. Can I get it?'

Kelena's head appeared through the hatch and nodded. 'Yes of course.' She withdrew and they grinned as they heard her start to shout at Petra.

Sarah recognised Ricki's voice and pressed the scrambler. 'Have you heard from London?' he asked.

'Yes, we're to sit tight and let them go ahead, in fact they want the goods to reach the UK, then they'll make arrests all along the line in one go. Janus is keeping our recording away from the office staff because of this *contact*, Podolski mentioned.'

Ricki interrupted. 'So it got through … amazing.'

She paused and glared at the receiver. 'Of course it got through,' conveniently forgetting her comment of surprise with Janus. 'He's spreading a rumour that he's pulling you out. If Johnnie becomes aware, then we do have a problem in London. I've already spoken to Panos this morning and he's going to have word with Petra to persuade him to take that job.'

'So you've brought Panos into this?'

'I don't think I have a choice.' She grinned to herself. 'He wants me to stay there ... in his Spiti.'

'What!'

'Well why not! He's very attractive.' She heard the explosion at the other end. 'Don't worry, I'm not that stupid.' She mused to herself looking at the receiver. *Jealous ... interesting.*

His voice calmed down, 'any sign of Podolski?'

'No, they didn't get in until half-one and sounded drunk.'

'I was frozen, sitting in the car, listening to that rain, waiting for them to leave ...' He paused. 'Thinking of you all snug in a warm bed...' She was aware of the noticeable pause. 'In the end, Henry and Johnnie carried Podolski to the car with that Danni holding an umbrella. What a pantomime! One moment they nearly dropped him over the bridge. I sat there willing him over.'

'You have a macabre sense of humour.'

'Of course I have! You need it in this job.'

'Keep your ears open to see if Johnnie gets a tip off.'

'Don't forget I've still got that bug hidden near the lounge.'

'Bye.'

After her breakfast she returned to her room but decided to be on the terrace when Podolski appeared. She felt she should draw him out. Returning downstairs, she selected a book from the hotel library donated by past holidaymakers. She kept shaking her head at the banal choice but chuckled and selected *Our Girl in Greece...a story of espionage!* She made herself comfortable on a lounger and started to read the first chapter with an expectant and bated breath.

Panos wandered in acknowledging her with a smile. He passed

into the bar and she could see him in deep conversation with Petra as they opened a bottle of Metaxa. Geraldine and Harold came in and paused with their beach towels. The woman stooped down to look at the book title. 'Oh dear, the stories they write today. Do you like spy stories my dear?'

Sarah turned the front over and studied at the title. 'I found it on the shelf ... seemed a bit of harmless holiday fun.'

Geraldine clasped both hands together. 'I've always had this fantasy of being a glamorous spy. You know, the Martini in one hand and the obligatory gold cigarette-holder in the other; looking mysterious and desirable; with a foreign accent of course. But Harold says I talk too much and couldn't keep a secret.'

The three laughed and she continued, 'I suspect you are a spy Sarah; a beautiful young girl on her own with these mysterious young men at your disposal.'

Harold interrupted and pulled her arm. 'Come on Geraldine; leave the young girl to enjoy her book. No, you'd never make a spy.' He raised his straw hat to Sarah and they wandered off towards the beach and the sun.

A few minutes later Panos emerged from the bar; his look suggested mission accomplished as he made his way towards the port. She sighed but kept re-reading the same page until she found tiredness catching up with the stress of the past few days. Her eyes became heavy and her thoughts kept drifting back to her brief time with Phillip; the walk after lunch and then the bitter goodbye. She tried to push the memory away but became aware of that voice again; the high-pitched croak of Shumonko Podolski.

She opened her eyes to see him and Danni standing at their table; Podolski staring at her. He moved across to stand over her with his presence bearing down. Her hand slipped into her open bag on the floor and touched the berretta to feel its comfort. She looked at this grotesque man; his baggy pink shorts and flour-white thin legs with red patches of sunburn, supporting his ridiculous body. He wore a *Brooklyn-Dodgers* shirt covering the heavy waist; his glistening bald head, mottled red from the sun, cheap whisky perspiration trickling down his face from the evening before; the podgy fingers gripping his straw hat; the other hand wiping a tissue across his wet face.

He looked down at her with his narrow expressionless eyes. 'Good morning Miss ... err ... Athina-Beaumont I think you call yourself.' He croaked, 'what are you reading?' He focused his eyes on the title and the fleshy mouth parted in a curled lip smile, giving a hissing imitation of laughter; she felt vulnerable and helpless under his crushing obscenity. Danni busied himself adjusting the cutlery on the table, occasionally glancing across, and then pulling out Podolski's chair he stood waiting for the man, his head inclined to one side, a look of bored resignation on his face?

Podolski asked, 'are you here for some time or is this a short break from the dampness of London?'

Sarah felt her hackles rise and she looked coldly up at the man above her. 'Depends, Mister Podolski, depends.'

He raised his thin, almost indiscernible ginger eyebrows. 'So you know my name then?'

'I'm surprised you know mine,' she answered coldly, 'we haven't spoken before.'

'I like to show an interest in my fellow travellers,' he hissed.

'But a fellow traveller usually means a person who shares the same interests of oneself. And I can't imagine sharing your interests Mister Podolski. In fact I would guess we are on opposite sides.'

His chilling blank eyes half closed and his features minacious. 'I always win Miss Athina-Beaumont,' he snapped, turning on his heels and shuffling back to his table as Kelena came in.

'Good morning Mister Podolski ... Danni.' She glanced across at Sarah and winked. Sarah pulled her hand from her bag and breathed more easily; round one?

Half way through their breakfast she tried not to notice Danni getting up and moving into the bar where he opened a bottle of Metaxa for Petra.

'... a Sarabande for Anna on the beach'

Sarah spent the rest of the day on the beach, swimming and hiding under a large deep-red sunshade, thinking about London and Phillip ... and Ricki ... she tried to pretend she didn't want him next to her on the beach ... and his quick reaction to her staying with Panos; she warmed to his apparent jealousy?

Panos watched her through his binoculars and curious as to why she kept her loose top on to go swimming. He wondered at her pulled muscle, and the visit of her doctor friend? There seemed to be a lot more she wasn't telling him. So she was born in Athens and speaking fluent Greek; oh dear had he said anything in jest she could have overheard? Would take refuge in his Spiti? He fingered his worry beads and thought of the conversation with Petra that morning. Petra was suspicious of course, his narrow island mind always suspicious; his dark, worn craggy face, and his brooding eyes trying to focus on his friend Panos, the brandy beginning to have its dulling conclusion. But his eyes had lit up at the suggestion of money, and yes he would pretend to be suspicious when approached by Danni; where money was concerned he would be good as his word. Panos knew he would play ball as Petra relied on his boat for spending money as Kelena always kept a tight grip on the hotel purse.

Sarah relaxed and focused on her spy novel. She read with amusement the action happening with every page. The heroine having an air of allure, romance and excitement as described by Geraldine that morning; but sadly, no long gold-plated cigarette holder. However she did have a handsome fellow agent called Wayne at her beck-and-call with an intriguing scar down one cheek. She smiled to herself. 'Sorry Ricki; you won't do ... no intriguing scar!'

She must have drifted off to sleep as the sudden blast from the ferry made her jerk, the book dropping on the sand. She automatically glanced at her watch and looked around. Harold was standing up to his knees in the water watching Geraldine gently swimming diligently in circles, her highly-flowered bathing cap in contrast to the deep blue of the Ionian Sea. Podolski was fast asleep on his back under the comfort of an umbrella, his mouth open, his hands resting on his rising and falling stomach; Danni sitting under his umbrella engrossed in a magazine. She studied the young man and wondered how he would waste his time in the company of such a disagreeable human being; she felt a curious intuition about him, something just didn't add up. He must have felt her gaze because he suddenly glanced in her direction. For one brief second their eyes locked but she quickly turned her head away. Several faces she recognised as coming from the hotel, but they were still strangers; people wanting to be private, keeping themselves to themselves. Her wound was aching, probably from her swimming exertion, so she washed some tablets down with her bottled water.

She picked up her book and tried to continue reading but her mind was on the evening ahead. She stared out to sea and watched the *Hellas Athina* on its return trip to Piraeus. She would contact Ricki and arrange for him to pick her up and go back to the woods overlooking the bay at Ingissi. It had a good view of the fishing quay and the waste container; they should be able to watch Petra and Danni return with the cargo. She glanced at her watch and picked up her bag and belongings. She waved to Harold and as she walked along the beach she sensed Danni's eyes burning into her back.

Kelena was humming to herself in the kitchen when Sarah looked round the door. 'Hi. What are we having tonight?'

Kelena smiled as she continued preparing vegetables and stated, 'Spetzofai.'

'Ah, I can recall that dish from my youth; it's spicy sausage, yes?'

'Yes ... and other things of course. It's very popular with the guests. There's always one that asks for the recipe. Would you like a pot of tea?'

Sarah nodded.

'I shall put the kettle on then.'

Sarah grabbed the kettle. 'No. I will put the kettle on, you are busy enough.'

'Thank you. You are a very good woman. Since you come here Sarah, I ask myself, why you have no man in your life. You seem to have good friends, but no lover?' She leaned with one hand on her kitchen knife pressed into the table and the other hand on her hip, anxious for an answer, watching the young woman who looked back with her intriguing eyes.

Sarah seemed taken aback with the question and slowly shook her head. 'I think my parents have given up on me. A married friend once suggested she has things that I don't have, but equally, I have a life she longs for.'

Kelena aware of Sarah becoming distant in her eyes as she continued quietly as if to herself, 'somehow I always knew my life would be this way, and I accepted it. I know it's what she wants until that time she releases me, which I feel is soon.' She suddenly turned to stare at Kelena, speaking sharply, 'can't have it all, can we? Guess I'm too fussy.'

Kelena tried to make sense with the answer but waved her knife. 'Well I got married too early and ended up with Petra.' She glared thoughtfully at the knife. 'I wouldn't wish him on anyone. He's stretching my patience today; getting under my feet; wanders around muttering to himself. He's up to something ... I can read him like a book.' Her face lightened. 'Now you go and sit down and I'll bring the tea.'

She laughed and attacked the vegetables with her sharp knife, thinking about Petra, pondering on the answer from the English girl.

Sarah kept the phone box door open with her back; was it to let fresh air in or the warm stale air out, she pondered as she waited, counting the number of rings and about to give up when Ricki answered.

She related her encounter with Podolski, and then suggested he picked her up late evening to watch Petra and Danni come in with the cargo. 'We can wait in the woods where we were before.'

'Will I get an ornithology lecture thrown in?'

'Probably.'

'If I recall, the liaison with the cargo boat was midnight so they should be back about one or one-thirty. How did Panos get on with Petra?'

'I haven't spoken to Panos but they appeared to have a long chat in the bar this morning, and after breakfast I saw Danni talking to Petra.' She lowered her voice a tone. 'Kelena has just told me that Petra seems on edge as if he's up to something.'

'Tell you what; I'll meet you at that bar in the side street just off the beach. It's called ... would you believe, *Zorba the Greek!*'

'That's original. OK,' she conceded. 'I'll be there about ten.'

'We've still got that drink money from Johnnie to spend if you remember,' came his reply before the phone went dead.

Sarah replaced the receiver. 'It'll be nice to get home and use the phone without these damn gadgets.' She then took a deep breath, dropping them into her bag.

That evening the hotel was full for dinner. Podolski and Danni dined in, ignoring her. The Spetzofai was a great success and Kelena took the compliments with a broad grin. And yes, she was correct, it happened to be Geraldine who asked for the recipe. Sarah caught Kelena's eye they shared the same thought. *It would have to be Geraldine.*

Sarah strolled through the small town down to the front. The evening air warm and soft; the inky night infinite with luminous stars and a floating moon; Saturn climbing in the south east; a calm sea with its gentle lapping. She passed the Spiti where she had shared a mug of coffee that morning with Panos, staring at the light in his window. Although she had taken the remark of his wife's running-off with slight amusement, she now felt a twinge of guilt. Since she had arrived on the island her life as a single girl had been questioned, not only by Kelena, but by the appearance of Phillip; and now here she was having a date with this Ricki; and she was choosy with what to wear this evening; did she want to be attractive for him? But then it wasn't really a date, or was it? Is this how her life has been mapped out? She suddenly felt lonely and despite the warm air, a chill went up her back. She pulled her light coat tighter and looked at her watch from the glow of a busy tavern. The few bars were alive with couples and families laughing and clinking glasses. Some children rushed past to the beach playing chase and catch, just like she and Michael used to. She felt nostalgic and wished she was back at Periandron Avenue. She was a fool for not letting Phillip kiss her, even though she was only a child; maybe her life would have been completely different. *Oh Katie for heaven's sake, pull yourself together; Phillip is the past.*

Above the holiday babble she became drawn to a rhythmic harmonica sound coming from the direction of rocks silhouetted at the end of the beach. She frowned, *could it be?* she wondered, taking off her shoes to walk across the warm sand to the shadowy figure. She paused to listen; pleasantly surprised. He became aware of her presence and stopped. He turned to gaze at the woman in the moonlight intently watching him.

Sarah whispered, 'don't stop. That was lovely. What is it?'

He jumped down from the rock and came to her. 'Bach. He dedicated the Sarabande to his wife Anna as she loved to dance and sing. Must have been a romantic old softie I guess ... I adapted it for the harmonica; don't know that he would approve of course.'

She found herself warming to him. 'Well I approve. I'm sorry to stop you. It's delightful and I think you play it beautifully. I'm seeing another side to you.'

'I was sitting there and thinking how romantic it would have seemed to her, Anna, the moon light; the view from a Greek island; me serenading her. Well it would have been with a girl next to me.'

They stood silent, gazing out to sea waiting for the other to break the spell.

Sarah suddenly put her arm through his. 'Come on Larry Adler, you and Johnnie are supposed to be buying me a drink. Remember?'

They paused at the path to wipe the sand from her bare feet. She stared along the path. 'Oh no, it's Geraldine and Harold. I don't want to be seen together tonight. She'll put two and two together and make five.'

He glanced at the approaching couple absorbed in the fairy tale night sky. He quickly turned his back on them; grabbing Sarah he kissed her firmly on the lips becoming aware of her perfume. She gasped and tried to push him away but suddenly relaxed as the interlopers passed, discreetly looking away from the young lovers.

She slowly, and he sensed reluctantly, pulled away exclaiming, 'you're taking liberties Ricki, whatever your name is.'

'Ricki Blane. All in the line of duty, ma'am,' shrugging his shoulders. 'Janus says when in a tight corner we must use our initiative.'

They walked on and into the Zorba with him trying to hide his silly grin and Sarah confused with the music and that *kiss*! Heading for a corner table he pulled a chair out, and as she sat down he bent forward and kissed her again on her cheek.

She feigned surprise. 'You're getting presumptuous Ricki.'

'I couldn't help myself,' he said, now openly grinning. He made a show of looking her over. 'Well I must say, you scrub up nicely, ma'am.'

She tried to look hurt, unsure now of her feelings for him. 'You certainly have an eloquent way with words when it comes to women.'

He admired her in the soft pinkish glow of the overhead lights.

He noticed for the first time, a slight hint of lipstick. 'Did you put that on for me?'

She frowned and he continued, ' ... the lipstick. Never seen you wear it before.'

'No, of course not,' she fibbed, trying not to catch his eyes.

He lit and pulled on his cigarillo and suddenly paused, waving his smoke. 'Sorry do you mind?'

She shook her head. 'Sorry about throwing your cigar over the edge like that. I shouldn't have done it.'

He mocked a hurt expression. 'Actually when you're angry, your eyes are very attractive, so I enjoyed it.'

She blushed and looked away enjoying the power within her eyes. Quickly changing the subject and noticing the barman looking across for their order. 'I'm getting rather thirsty. Where's this drink you and Johnnie keep promising?' she demanded.

She had wanted to talk about the evening ahead and all that had happened over the past few days, but now she didn't want to; she should give more time to enjoying herself. Since her time on the island she hadn't thought of Ricki other than work, but now felt drawn to the man sitting opposite. He was quite handsome really and she was beginning to enjoy his presence; it had nothing to do with that unexpected kiss of course! Making conversation she asked, 'how long have you worked for the department and Janus?'

He had to give the question some thought. 'I've been with the department for about two years, and about one year ago, after seeing you come and go, disappearing for a month at a time, which all seemed glamorous and exciting, I began to hanker after something more than a desk job. So I applied to Janus personally. He must have thought I was ...' he imitated Janus, '"*a jolly good chap*" because he sent me down to "*the delights of Hedge Farm, hedge trimming and eradicating undesirable weeds.*"'

Sarah giggled. 'Just like him! Have you ever done that to his face?'

Ricki's face dropped in horror. 'I daren't. He's God!'

She was starting to relax; 'I can't remember you in the

department,' which wasn't true of course. 'Where did you work and why haven't we met before?'

He continued her game. 'You never came into our department. We weren't in Janus's pecking order. You didn't know I existed. I wasn't even on your radar. You were one of Janus's luvvies. Stuck up I thought.' He watched her face and burst out laughing.

Her eyes glared and she slapped the table. 'Stuck up, damn cheek. I thought you were an arrogant little sod. No wonder I didn't want to talk to you.'

'Oh.' He raised his eyebrows. 'You said you didn't know I existed.'

They both sat in silence sipping their drinks until Sarah burst out laughing; she hadn't enjoyed flirtatious banter like this for a long time. He continued, 'I know he took you to lunch once and I sat there having my soggy sandwiches and drinking office coffee ... not that I was jealous.'

She puckered her lips and her eyes glinted. 'You were jealous because he didn't take *you* ...' Her face became enquiring and she threw down the gauntlet, '... or because he took *me*?'

He paused, weighing up his options, but crumbled. 'Yes, because he took you. Why should he get all the luck, just because he's God ... that's no excuse.' He tried to be serious. 'So when I realised it was you who had sneaked on the island behind my back, I decided I would do my own sneaking and catch you out. Teach you a lesson.'

'... and who had the lesson?' she demanded through clenched teeth and a challenging look.

He raised both hands in surrender. 'OK, round one to you.' He wagged his finger. 'There'll be other times.'

A sudden, high-pitched giggle turned their heads to glance down the road as Panos approached with a young blond bombshell clutching his arm. He turned and entered into their tavern not noticing the two watching with amusement. They headed for the bar corner and Panos sat her at a far table whispering in her ear. She put her hand to his mouth and squealed again. He straightened up and suddenly spotted the two staring faces. For a moment he didn't know whether to accept defeat or to disappear into the bar.

He finally bowed to the inevitable and came over. They detected a slight flush on his neck.

Ricki smiled at him. 'Well, Panos you certainly know how to pick them. Was it her mind that first attracted you, or was it her captivating laugh?'

Sarah stifled a guffaw with her hand.

Panos glanced back at the girl as she admired her long red nails. 'Yes she can be a bit trying,' he admitted.

Sarah smiled and commented, 'don't tell me you're going to take her home and read *Homer's Iliad* to her. She would be enthralled to hear all about Achilles and his poor heel.'

His face broke into a lop-sided grin. 'Well it would be interesting.'

Ricki looked puzzled. '*Homer's Iliad?*'

Sarah tried to look serious. 'Surely there has to be a Cockney slang for that Ricki ... No?'

Panos looked at his watch. 'What's going to happen later tonight?' He glanced at Sarah. 'I imagined you might go up there?'

'That's why Ricki's come to pick me up. We're just enjoying a drink.'

With a hint of jealousy in his voice Panos mumbled sharply, 'I could have taken you.'

Sarah glanced at the blond girl. 'I wouldn't dream of taking you away from your evening's entertainment, Panos.'

Just then the girl squealed and the three looked across at the barman whispering in her ear.

Ricki shook his head. 'I think you better get back, you've got competition.'

Panos glared at the barman and quickly said to Sarah, 'I might see you later,' and scurried across to the girl. He pulled her up and they hurried off to the neighbouring tavern as she squealed, protesting and staggering on high heels over the stony road.

Sarah grinned at Ricki and looked at her watch. 'I better go back to the hotel and change. Meet me in about thirty minutes near the Beachcomber bar.'

He nodded, eyeing her up and down. 'The effort was appreciated,'

117

he said warmly.

She glanced down and adjusted her hair. 'I didn't do anything special,' she fibbed again.

He grinned shaking his head. 'No, of course not.' *Where had he heard that line before?*

'... *the midnight cargo*'

Ricki switched off the Escort's lights as it swung from the road on-to the familiar track they had driven two evenings before; the bright moonlight enough to guide him as he pulled into the same position. They sat in silence for a while admiring the shadowy view looking over Ingissi Island and onto the distant, moon-painted horizon, beginning to show ominous gathering dark streaks of cloud; the sounds of crickets enveloping the woods. Sarah sighed. 'That reminds me of my childhood in Athens, lying in bed trying to get to sleep on a hot night; so evocative.' She took a deep breath. '*Orthoptera* ... that's their name, should you be interested.'

Ricki muttered, 'if you say so. I could kill the little blighters some nights, trying to get to sleep.'

'Philistine,' was her acerbic reply as she got out of the car and moved to the edge with her night glasses. She scanned the little harbour taking in the few pickups of the fishermen already out at sea. There was one boat just leaving, turning away from its berth and then chugging out of the little harbour causing splashing sounds on the jetty. The distant pop-pop of its diesel carried across the small bay until it too dissolved into the night. She could just make out dark shapes of the numerous stationary fishing boats in the distance; some with gas lamps alight at the stern, drawing in the fish. Occasionally there was a tapping noise from the direction of the boats. Ricki appeared beside her and whispered, 'they're attracting the octopus; some nights if the wind is from that direction, it drives me mad ... and I hate octopus.'

Suddenly the island light came on and they focused their glasses on Henry feeding the dog. He then pushed open the grating gate, and waited holding a tin. They heard him call out and Johnnie appeared behind him. Henry led with a torch as the island sensor light shut off. They both hurried over the bridge to two skips on the quay and started to remove rubbish from one of them.

Ricki leaned over, enjoying her nearness, aware her perfume had gone after her visit to the hotel and whispered, 'tonight we have two skips ... interesting ... notice the jetty light is switched off ... for a purpose of course.'

The two men spent time peering inside and appeared to be discussing one of the containers. Henry then opened the tin and Johnnie stood back as Henry threw a liquid against the side. Johnnie shone a torch on the liquid; it was bright red. Sarah whispered, 'of course, that's paint to mark the container. It looks as though it's been spilt.' She looked at Ricki. 'Better than putting an obvious mark, he's not daft. I was going to get Panos to identify it for us, now there's no need. All the fishing boats have left, so Petra and Danni must be out there somewhere.' She twisted her watch to catch the moon. 'It's midnight! They should be meeting up with the ship about now.' They both scanned the horizon concentrating for signs of movement. Suddenly Ricki pointed to a dark shape almost out of their view, partially obscured near the headland displaying navigation lights, the ship itself remained in darkness. He murmured, 'that's a large vessel. It's not a fishing boat, bet that's it.'

They both were startled by rustling behind them and Sarah gasped as her leg was nudged by a wet nose together with the dull clang of a goat's bell. In the moonlight two startled shiny eyes stared at the strangers. They tried not to burst out laughing.

Ricki waved his arms. He whispered, 'go away. Shoo!'

The startled animal tore off through the undergrowth, its bell clanging into the distance.

He chuckled. 'That'll be interesting at your debriefing.'

They heard a car moving down to the harbour and the headlights of the taxi appeared swinging across the bay with the sound of crunching tyres breaking the stillness. For one brief moment it illuminated Johnnie and Henry who threw up their hands from the glare. It parked and the lights went off. The driver Ivan got out and stood with his back to the car. He lit a cigarette and watched the two men walk over. Suddenly the rear door opened and the inside light revealed Podolski who struggled to pull his large frame out; he didn't have Danni there to help him out this night; nobody else offered, they noticed. The four men stood in a circle, occasionally glancing out to sea. Podolski refusing a cigarette and the scene remained a ghoulish dream set in the moonlight with just the infrequent orange cigarette glow across the faces.

Sarah jumped and ducked as a Vesper bat brushed across her head. Ricki caught her and they both silently laughed. He held her for a moment. 'Alright?'

She shivered. 'Sorry. I could feel the wind as it passed ... made me jump. Tonight I've been attacked by a demented musician on the beach, a wet nosed goat and now a bat; what next I wonder?' She didn't move his arm away, causing him to whisper, 'when we get back to London maybe we could meet up for lunch?'

She nodded. 'Maybe.' She pushed him away. 'Let's wait till this job's over.'

They occasionally heard Podolski's high pitched voice rising from the bay. The crickets seemed to be getting louder and more bats started swooping. They thought they heard a car in the distance with the sound stopping as quickly as it came. 'Wonder who that is?' whispered Ricki. They strained to listen above the crickets as the crunch of approaching footsteps sounded behind them. Sarah gripped her Beretta and dropped behind a tree. Ricki disappeared into the night; she guessed he would be on the other side of the track. A moonlit figure appeared who looked into the car. She recognised the features of Panos who froze as he felt the cold steel of the Beretta against his neck. He croaked, 'it's only me ... Panos.'

'Thought you would have been reading *Homer* to the girlfriend by now?'

He turned and looked into the shadowy face of Sarah. 'Hell, you made me jump. Look I'm shaking. Where's your boyfriend then?'

He jumped as he felt Ricki's hand on his shoulder. 'Right behind you, you're losing your touch, Panos. Too much romancing I reckon. Where's your goat then?'

The newcomer pulled out a handkerchief and wiped his face. 'What goat?'

Ricki whispered, 'and where's Marilyn Monroe?'

He looked sheepish and scowled, lowered his voice to a whisper, 'I went to get another drink and when I came back she was climbing onto that barman's moped, waving and giggling as they took off. I'll kill him. I'll never get drunk in his bar again!'

Sarah felt herself shaking with suppressed laughter and turned away.

Just then they caught raised voices from below with the low humming drone of a diesel engine coming into the small harbour. They focused their binoculars onto a shadowy fishing boat bumping against the jetty. A moon silhouetted figure, looking like Danni, stood on the bow; he threw a rope to the waiting group. It was Henry who caught and tied it to a bollard; the diesel left running. Sounds of talking and laughter, interrupted by Podolski's high pitched voice urging them on. They busied themselves off-loading bags from the boat. These were carried and placed carefully into the metal skip with Henry's voice warning them about the wet paint. The rubbish was thrown back in and they stood awhile talking and pointing in the direction of the cargo ship that had now disappeared into the night. Petra jumped into his boat and Henry untied the rope throwing it back on board. The engine revved and Petra reversed out before swinging the bow towards the open sea; back to his fishing anchorage before he was missed by his fellow fishermen.

Danni helped Podolski back into the taxi, hurrying round to the other side to sit in the front seat. The taxi quickly reversed and shot forward, its lights vanishing behind the trees, only the sound of tyres crunching on gravel, its engine revving before fading into the night behind them. Johnnie and Henry crossed the bridge suddenly illuminated by the sensor light from the island. Henry closed and locked the gate with its irritating squeak, quietly talking to the dog before following Johnnie into the villa. The light went off; all was still, as if the harbour was catching its breath before the first wave of fishing boats returned at dawn with their night's catch. With the crickets continuing their constant sound, the tapping out at sea suddenly stopped and the three watchers remained silent until Sarah angled her watch at the moon, whispering over the crickets, 'one-thirty! Well I don't know about you gentlemen, but I'm off to my bed.'

Ricki cut in. 'I think we should go back and show ourselves. I want them to think I was in town all the time. Especially as the taxi driver is involved in this.'

Sarah nodded. 'You're right. We'll give you a lift to your car Panos.' She noticed his obvious disappointment at not taking her back into town, so she offered, 'Ricki can buy us both a drink and we can discuss *Homer*.' His gloomy face changing into a grin.

'... *juridicum dies non*'

After a restless night probably caused by that kiss, she sensed a delicious idleness spreading through her limbs, wanting sleep to decide her getting-up time. She was in no hurry, she had done her job and the rest was now up to Janus. She peered at her watch, seven-fifteen, she stretched and turned over. Her time on the island was now coming to an end and Janus had suggested she should relax and soak up the sun; was he buttering her up, trying to prepare her for Sarajevo? His main concern was Podolski and his threat to her; his advice, *announce to Kelena that she will be leaving in a couple of days and make sure Geraldine knew.* Podolski would soon hear and assume she was of no further threat and his arrangements with Johnnie would be fruitful with his new contacts in London. The flap caused with the death of the agent a week before had suddenly gone quiet. Janus would now be careful and impart false information to confuse Podolski's London contact and that could be quite useful; her mind going round and round.

She eventually sat up and felt her side. The wound was healing well and doubted if she would have much of a scar, thanks to Ricki immediately using the plaster strips to pull the wound together … *Ricki, who would have thought she could feel a need for him? Nothing to do with the kiss of course!* She wrinkled her nose. *So he thought I was stuck up did he? Damn cheek* … but then she did tell him he was arrogant … *well he is* … yes she would like to meet up again back in London, outside of the office in their own time. Perhaps they'll go back to what it was before as two strangers in the office?

Maybe he was leading her on? London can be so grey away from a sunny and heavenly Greek island. The thought occurred to her that Phillip hadn't been in her mind over night. Was it because of Ricki? She pulled the curtains back and opened the door to step onto the balcony. There was already living warmth in the early morning sun and it felt sensuous as it bathed her body. Outside the harbour, the dark blue sea had become choppy and white, and the gentle warm breeze coming up from Africa suggested a mood change in the weather.

She felt a need to go for a long walk to clear her head. She knew that once she was in London it would be straight back on the treadmill. Not long ago she would have jumped at the chance to sneak into Sarajevo, even with the obvious danger involved; now she was unsure. Apart from when she went down to her parents in Devon, she didn't have any opportunity to walk through woods and fields, so she must ask Kelena for a packed lunch and have the whole day on her own. She had to make up her mind whether she should take that job as an instructor at Hedge Farm. She was fully aware that Janus would try to talk her out of it. She was beginning to have doubts with her present position anyway. She recalled her mentor at Hedge saying, *"should you ever get doubts, then that's when you must leave field work; that's when you start making mistakes"*. Had she made mistakes on this trip? She needed someone close to confide in, but there wasn't anyone; *had Athina abandoned her?* Suddenly she smelt bacon and coffee; she was hungry.

Podolski and Danni were already at their table. They both glanced up but she ignored them and looked into the kitchen and was greeted by a smiling Kelena. 'You always have such a lovely smile Kelena. I don't know how you keep it going with all this hard work?'

She laughed. 'For you Sarah, there will always be a smile.'

Sarah asked for a packed lunch, and then told her that she would be leaving in a couple of days.

Kelena's face dropped and she put her arms around her. 'Promise me, you will return?'

Sarah nodded feeling sad to be leaving this good woman and then she thought of all the good people who had passed through her life as Sarah, but she had to forget them because of her job; they wouldn't know her as herself ... as Katie.

As she waited for her breakfast, she was aware that Podolski was in an unusually jovial mood but kept her gaze from him. Geraldine and the faithful Harold entered as Kelena brought her breakfast to the table. She put her arm across Sarah's shoulders and announced, 'I'm afraid we're going to lose this lovely English lady. Sadly she is going back home.'

Geraldine smiled at Sarah. 'But you've had lovely quiet time here. This is the perfect place to comfort the matters of the heart.'

Sarah blinked and noticed Harold nudging, pulling her to their table. 'Come my dear, Sarah is trying to eat her breakfast.'

Geraldine widened her smile and gave a knowing wink to Sarah, who felt the sides of her mouth twitching.

She decided to walk in another direction towards the Southern spur of the island. She didn't notice Podolski watching, his face darkened as he turned and spoke to Danni. She was aware Janus told her not to go anywhere quiet on her own after that threat from Podolski; stick to the town he stated. But she desperately needed the solitude she always drew from nature. Just be an ordinary person again, enjoying the peace and quiet away from the crazy world she found herself in. She was pleased she remembered to bring her walking shoes on this trip as the gravel road was unstable and sloped upwards. The road swept through a variety of trees and fauna, so she opened her favourite must-bring travel accessory, Dobinson's Index of Fauna & Native Trees. She acknowledged a Tamarisk next to a Carob, plenty of recognisable giant Eucalyptus, the umbrella branches giving welcome dappled shelter from the hot sun and covering the area next to the cliff edge. She identified a Ficus carica, with its recognisable large fig leaves. As she reached an opening with a sweeping vista of the deep blue sea, an acrid smell drifted in the warm air. Above came the sight and sound of screeching and soaring seagulls with the heavy buzz of swarming flies. The scene made her gasp and hold a hand across her mouth; this was the rubbish dump that Geraldine and Harold complained about; piles of torn black plastic bags strewn across the face of the cliff; the edges of the rubbish scarred from fires that the EEC had stopped, the air still acrid from the burnt plastic. She turned away and heard the crunch of tyres coming up the hill.

The island taxi pulled up, the rear window started to lower and she felt a sense of fear grip her stomach as she stared into the soulless eyes of Podolski. He face had a chilling, menacing look, and he opened the car door. She went to run but he waved a revolver in his hand. 'Stay where you are my *dear* woman,' his voice rising even more unnatural and feminine. He dragged his comical body out, looking even more grotesque with his strange straw hat and baggy shorts, advancing towards her as Danni came round from the front passenger seat and stood by his side; Ivan remained in the car, staring. Podolski sneered. 'So you thought you would ruin all my plans. Nobody takes anything away from me ... especially a *woman!*'

Sarah felt sick from the nauseating stench of rubbish and the heat, her heart was pounding. She desperately glanced around but there was no escaping this mad man.

His animal laugh became high pitched. 'What did Janus think he would achieve with sending you?' he snarled. Danni handed him a canvas bag and came over to pull off her backpack. For a moment, she stared deep into his dark brown eyes but he revealed no emotion. He opened the flap and pulled out her Beretta, he pushed it into his waistband and handed back her bag, pausing again to stare into her eyes as if he was trying to say something. She clasped it tightly in her trembling hands and could feel the sweat pouring down her body. She felt giddy and could sense the insane look behind Podolski's blank sockets, his madness; *what was this lunatic thinking?*

She pleaded to Danni with her eyes. Ivan was now drawing on a cigarette, quietly gazing at the scene. Her mind went to her parents, and Michael, and Phillip, and now Ricki, living their own lives, all unaware it was ending here at a rubbish tip. She closed her eyes, gave the sign of the cross and tried to close her mind; why has Athina abandoned her? The clown-like figure shuffled over to the edge and clasped a red handkerchief to his flaccid lips and nose. He turned and slowly raised the gun to her face throwing the bag at her feet. Her instinct was to lunge forward, but he was too far away. He motioned the gun towards the bag. 'Open it,' he demanded. She knelt down, her hand shaking as she pulled the zip; it held wads of drachmas.

'There is the equivalent of one hundred thousand of your English pounds. There's more if you want it,' he rasped. 'All women are whores and even sell their soul if the price is right. I don't want your body ... I want your soul because you *will* work for me in London.' She stared at the crazed man, her head spinning; he was completely insane. He moved closer, his face red. 'I can see in your eyes the greed of your species.' His voice rose and he screamed, 'you're all sluts. Take the money and work for me, damn you. Your soul, woman ...' He threw his head back, shrieking with laughter, screaming, 'your soul - damn you!'

She kicked the bag over the side, the canvas catching a rock and splitting with the paper money blowing into the hot wind rising up with the stench. She threw herself forward at him, screaming, 'go to hell!'

He raised the gun and fired but his arm jerked as another gun exploded and the clown figure of Podolski shuddered. He turned his head and stared at Sarah's Beretta in Danni's firm hand, and then at the smile on Danni's lips and the hatred in his narrowed eyes. The grotesque body rolled backwards, his unblinking sockets suddenly displaying an emotion of fear, he floated out and down into the rubbish, the red handkerchief still held against the lips, his strange straw hat floating away in the upward heat from the rotting mass; screeching seagulls scattering in panic with the clouds of flies spraying the air. The offensive stench overwhelming and dozens of rats suddenly appeared, squealing and scampering away. She watched the body sink, disappearing into the bottom of the dump as tonnes of disturbed stinking rubbish slid down, burying it forever. Thousands of notes continued to float and dance in the heat rising from the rotting waste. She sank to her knees and was violently sick. Tears rolling down her face as she felt two strong hands grip and pull her up. She couldn't focus, her eyes blurred, but she heard Danni's voice, 'come on, let's get out of this stinking hell and leave him to the rats.'

Her knees refused to move and he half carried her to the car. Ivan opened the rear door as Danni helped her in. He shouted to Ivan, 'Sa plecam de aici,' and jumped in the other side. He handed her a bottle of water as the car continued up the hill, the tyres spinning in the gravel. She gasped as the water flowed down her parched throat.

The car pulled into shade overlooking the town far below. Ivan got out and leaned back into the car offering a cigarette. Danni took one but Sarah shook her head so he put it in his shirt pocket. Ivan strolled away and rested against a towering eucalyptus, drawing on his cigarette, glancing occasionally at the couple now out of the car and sitting under a stone pine. Sarah inclined her back against the hard trunk, the sharp smell of the pine in contrast to the sweet aroma of the gum-cistus that dominated the island; but the acrid smell of the tip still in her nostrils. She was still shaking but slowly regained her composure before turning her face to look with drained eyes at her new companion. 'And who the hell are you?'

He motioned his cigarette. 'Do you mind?'

She shrugged her shoulders. 'I don't give a damn what you do.'

He lit up and stared out to sea. 'My name is Sergin Dimitri ... Inspectorul Sergin Dimitri of the Serviciul Român de Informatii.' He paused. 'Romanian Secret Service.' His voice had now changed to mid-European. 'I work personally for the Romanian Prime Minister. After we rid ourselves of Ceausescu, we thought it was going to be sunshine all the way, but now we watch our country slowly destroyed by these mafia gangs. We have very little money for this work so my President asked the French President for their assistance; I was assigned to work with a Capitainé Andre Herisson of their DGSE. We have known about Podolski for a number of years. I worked my way into Podolski's confidence. And my instructions were, when the time was right ...' he pointed his hand in the shape of a pistol, 'bang! Exterminate him!' He grimaced and waved his cigarette. 'What direct evidence could we get on him? Podolski always had others to do his dirty work, like that Ion. He was starting to get suspicious because things were going wrong for him so I guess it was only a matter of time before he turned on me. He could be vicious.' He stared at her with his deep brown eyes. 'You saved me a job. How is your wound?' She wouldn't answer. He blew a ring of smoke and they both watched the circle float out to sea. 'How did it happen?'

'I was searching Ion's room when he was supposed to be with Petra on his boat.'

'I see. You did a good cover up. I was impressed. Podolski really thought he had fallen over the cliff. I guessed different of course.' He laughed to himself. 'I've seen it too many times to be fooled.' They watched another smoke ring. 'No country would touch him. Even if Podolski was convicted, with our damn new, so called, liberal justice system, he would soon be out of prison to continue, and who would want to pick up the bill for a lengthy trial. The DGSE have a policy of exterminating these scum. It is the only way. Nobody cries at their funeral.' He gave a silent laugh and shrugged. 'But then nobody attends ... sad really. My instructions were to take him out at the right time.' He again waved his cigarette. 'Today was not the right time but I had no choice ... in the end of course, it was he who decided the time. He was mad!'

Sarah stared at the man. 'But ... why me? He knew I was leaving.'

He drew on the cigarette. 'Because you're a woman, and he thought he could buy your soul. OK. He was insane.' He raised his hands. 'He hated women. It is something to do with being abandoned in one of Ceausescu's orphanages. You've seen the pictures of the kids there and their conditions. How could they possibly grow into normal adults? He had no chance, and he was eaten by this obsession that he was put on earth as an insult to the human race by a woman who considered him too ugly to love, and so abandoned him in a gutter.'

That remark cut deep into Sarah's feelings.

'No woman could possibly be attracted to him; he was too disgusting. He felt it was a personal insult by Janus to send a female, especially a woman like you. He feared your beauty and so maybe he was frightened of you, and that is why he thought all he had to do was buy your soul like all the others. He was on the edge of madness and needed just one push to trigger him off; you appeared. In his warped mind you were deliberately sent by the English man Janus, as a jest.' He gave her an absorbing look and laughed. 'But you kicked his money away and that was sweet; it was counterfeit anyway and I'm only sorry to put you through all that down there.' He nodded in the direction of the tip. 'I tried to convey hope to you, and I wanted your gun. I prayed that you would be carrying one … here.' He pulled her Beretta from his waistband and dropped it into her bag. 'Take it, the job is done. I could not understand why you took the chance to go for a walk on your own. Only in pairs we had drummed into us. Cover each other's backs.'

She was silent for a while, he was right of course. She quietly asked, 'and what would have happened if I didn't have a gun?'

He indicated to Ivan. 'He had Podolski covered, but I wanted to dispatch him with your gun; thought you would appreciate the gesture.'

She looked over at Ivan. 'And who is he?'

'Sergeant Adrian Bochinsky. We have worked together for many years. I particularly asked for him. Podolski persuaded Christos to part with his taxi. Podolski was good at persuasion.' He rubbed his fingers together, ' … plenty of drachmas as well. It's the eyes and ears of the island. We like to keep an eye on the Russians here as well.'

He frowned and glanced at her. 'You realise I am here with the blessing of the Greek government?'

'No! We didn't know.'

'They're concerned with foreigners coming in with all this money. Nothing wrong with money but what it brings; these islands are perfect for their activities.' He shook his head and gestured the sea and the distant islands. 'Why does beauty have to attract evil?'

They remained silent, staring at the peaceful solitude laid out before them. Looking pensive he quietly murmured, *"'when sorrows come, they come not single spies—'"*

Sarah broke in, *"'but in battalions ... and as much containing as all, her brother is in secret come from France.'"* She looked at him, raising an eyebrow. 'Shouldn't that be Romania?'

He grinned. 'I'm impressed!'

She moved away from the hard pine to ease her now burning side. Looking earnestly at him, she asked, 'surely, it is I that should be impressed.' She inclined her head, querying him, 'Shakespeare from a Romanian?'

His lined face softened. 'No! Shakespeare belongs to the world. Unfair really how your God gave one Englishman all the best speeches,' and then he laughed.

The square lantern-jawed face of Sergeant Adrian Bochinsky watched the couple for a while, emotionally unmoved by the past hour; too scarred by his Romanian youth. He squatted to scowl through his heavy-lidded eyes at the antics of a spider moving in a circle around a ladybird. He blew a shaft of smoke at the insects; taunting, but the spider shot under a leaf leaving the ladybird to ignore the gesture, slowly crawling up a stick; a female defiant of man.

Sarah offered the bottle of water to Danni who gratefully swigged the nectar. She gave him a quizzical look. 'Why did you draw Podolski's attention to me, staying at the hotel?'

'When?'

'When you had your meeting at Johnnie's? When you discussed the cargo coming in?'

He paused at taking another drink. 'How did you know? Was

your agent Ricki listening?'

'He was with me. We were both listening from the cliff. Never mind how, but you *did* describe me.'

'Yes I did. Podolski was already suspicious of you.' He shrugged his shoulders. 'I had to go along with it. Anyway, it was what he paid me for.'

She retorted angrily, 'he tried to kill me!'

'But he didn't ...' He crushed his cigarette into the soil, '... and now *he's* dead like that cigarette!'

'And another question,' she said angrily. 'What was that business of trying my bedroom handle when you came in last night?'

He stared puzzled at her and then grinned. 'Sorry about that. Podolski was stupidly drunk and I left him whilst I switched on the next floor-light and he wandered trying the rooms. That must have given you a fright.'

'Yes, and he would have had a fright as I was in there with my gun.'

She wiped her moist eyes with the back of her hand causing him to look inquiringly as he then shook his head. 'I don't know why they send women for this type of work. You all get emotional.' His face hardened. He challenged her, 'why aren't you home with a family?'

Her anger flared and she turned on him. 'You're all chauvinists. All of you! You lived with that monster for too long; you're just like him! Because of you men, the world's in such a mess!' She stood up holding her aching side with one hand and leaned against the pine, demanding, 'take me back to the hotel!'

Inspectorul Sergin Dimitri of the Serviciul Român de Informatii rose to his feet, nodding at Sergeant Adrian Bochinsky.

As they drove back down the hill, she asked to stop at the tip. They watched from the car as she walked to the edge and looked over. The seagulls and flies had calmed down. There was a moment when she appeared to have her head bowed. She crossed herself before stepping back to the car. The surprised, yet bemused Inspectorul Sergin Dimitri leaned forward and pushed her door open. As she sat in he asked, 'why him? He doesn't need a prayer where he's going.'

'I don't suppose he has ever had a prayer spoken for him in his sad life; surely he deserves one in death.' She turned her strained face to him, asking, 'is there no charity in the soul of a man who purports to love Shakespeare?'

A shadow crossed his face, he bit his lip. 'If you had lived with us under the cruelty of Ceausescu, maybe your charitable soul would have been crushed like that cigarette!'

The car continued down to the hotel with the Romanian quiet, touched with her gesture to the man who had just tried to kill her. She sank back into the beer-reeking leather seat, her thoughts on his comment, *"why aren't you home with a family?"* She sighed, closing her eyes, tiredness draining her body. *He is right of course, why aren't I home with a family?*

She had never felt so alone and so miserable; but she also knew ... *Inspectorul Sergin Dimitri had been sent by Athina!*

'... *tomorrow, another day*'

Sarah dreaded meeting Geraldine, or even Kelena, but managed to go unseen straight to her room. Tearing off clothes, she showered away the odour and emotional fatigue of the past hours from her exhausted mind. As she felt the stinging hot water, her anger rose and she screamed, slapping the tiles in frustration and relief. 'You idiot Katie Simpson ... *you nearly blew it!*' She sank down, kneeling in the tray with the hot water cascading over her, helping to wash the past stinking hour down the drain. After a while, the water suddenly cooled and she reached up and turned it off. She wrapped the towel round her aching body and went into the bedroom to flop, weeping, on the bed. The tears flowed as she drifted into her disturbed sleep; the acrid smell still in her nostrils. She tried not to succumb to the devil, she kept trying to brush the flies away from her face ... the screeching of the seagulls and the crazy man laughing ... the gradual awareness of knocking at the door.

'Sarah ... Sarah are you there?'

She twisted round and looked at her watch ... *eight*. She rubbed her eyes. 'Who is it?'

'Ricki.' His voice concerned. 'You OK?'

The sun had now left the balcony in shadow and she became aware of voices drifting up from the restaurant, the occasional laughter and clink of glasses. She wrapped her towel tighter and opened the door. His anxious face looked her up and down.

'Come on in. You'll have to take me as you see me.' She sat down on the bed as he closed the door. He looked around the room and the discarded clothes lying on the floor. She stifled a yawn. 'I'm sorry but I must have crashed out.' She became silent and continued to stare at the tiled floor.

He sat down putting his arm around her. 'I met Danni, or whoever he is, and he told me what happened this morning. My God, Sarah, that was a narrow escape. What on earth made you go out like that?' He sounded angry. 'We agreed you should stay here, or no more than the town.'

'I had to go somewhere on my own. I needed to think.'

'I think you need me to look after you.'

She looked at his worried face, he was right she did want him to look after her, but she still couldn't, or want to admit it. She relented by resting her head on his shoulder and gripping his hand. 'I can't continue Ricki. I've never been so frightened in all my life. He is right; it's not woman's work.'

'Who said that?'

'That Danni. Said I should go home and have a family. Leave it to men.'

'Bloody chauvinist!

She laughed. 'That's what I said.'

He kissed her damp hair still smelling of soap. 'Are you hungry? 'cause I'm starving.'

She nodded. 'Yes, me too.' She put her hand to her mouth. 'Oh dear, I haven't eaten Kelena's lunch. Don't tell her, she'll be disappointed.'

He roared with laughter. 'Fancy thinking of that.'

'Where did you see Danni?'

'Downstairs. He's having a beer ... on his own of course. He invited us for a drink. He says he wants to apologise.'

Her face flared and she bristled. 'So he should!'

He laughed. 'That's my Sarah. Look, I'll leave you to dress. See you downstairs.' He stood and looked down at her still holding her hand. 'Can't I call you Katie?'

'I don't even know your name. Oh God, what stupid games we play for Janus ... for heaven's sake.'

'Andrew. I prefer Andy.'

He bent down and kissed her head, wiping the tears from her cheeks.

She smiled and squeezed his hand. 'See you in a minute Andy.'

As he went to close the door she asked him, 'why Ricki?'

He grinned. 'My favourite film ... Casablanca.'

Sarah frowned. 'Casablanca?'

'Yeah ... Bogart played Rick Blane ... seemed a natural choice.' He called back, 'love the freckles.'

She glanced in the mirror, *freckles?* Touching her face ... *where?* 'Don't be cheeky,' she shouted ... *and then remembered the body submerged in the tip; it could have been her.* 'Sod you Podolski,' she screamed at the echoic room.

The two men stood as she came into the bar. They both gazed at the woman walking towards them wearing a simple cream dress, her hair loose and shiny; with just a hint of lipstick; the colour matching the beads round her neck and the drop earrings and her sling-back evening shoes. She paused for a moment as they looked her up and down. 'Well gentlemen, do I have to buy my own drink?'

Inspectorul Sergin Dimitri moved forward and kissed her hand. *"Foreswear its sight ... for I never saw true beauty 'til this night."* They noticed a slight blush come to her cheeks. He smiled. 'You look a different woman to this morning, but please forgive me for my stupid and unnecessary outburst earlier. You looked so vulnerable and finished. I was wrong.' He still held her hand.

She smiled and nodded. 'Of course Sergin; but you saved my life. I will forever be grateful. Thank you.' She leaned forward and kissed his cheek.

He grinned and looked at Ricki. 'See what you have to do to get a kiss from this young lady?'

Sarah whispered loudly, 'I'm saving his for when we get back to London.'

Ricki tried to hide his silly grin by looking away at Kelena coming from the restaurant carrying a tray. She raised her eyebrows at the group. She looked at Danni and nodded. 'Your table for three is ready.' She smiled at Sarah and continued into the kitchen where they heard her shout. Petra appeared and ambled to the bar to pour Sarah a gin and tonic. She leaned over the bar and whispered in Greek, 'I need to talk to you in the morning. Make sure you're around.' He stared at her stony expression, his craggy face unsure, but he slowly nodded in a worried agreement.

The three went into the restaurant and Sarah was amused by Geraldine watching from the far corner, ears itching for news. As Kelena came to their table with the menu, she asked Danni, 'when do you think Mr. Podolski will be returning?'

He raised his face, his eyes narrowed and distant. 'Shumonko Podolski? Sometimes I wonder if he ever existed.' He grimaced at Kelena's puzzled expression. 'He is an enigma and I fear he has a date with the devil.'

Sarah bit her lip and kept her face down, staring at the menu; aware Geraldine's ears must be working overtime. Kelena looked at the new Sarah. 'You should be taken out for dinner more often, it does wonders for you. What I really mean,' her eyes twinkled with mischief, 'it does wonders for the men.'

After she had moved to another table, Ricki spoke quietly to her, 'your Uncle Alec will be ringing tomorrow morning.'

Sarah sighed and turned the menu page. 'Ricki Blane. Tomorrow is another day. I need to get today over with.'

Danni looked at Ricki's face and grinned.

Just then Panos entered. He froze when he saw them and then strolled across to their table. Sarah must have sensed him as she didn't even look up from the menu, but held the palm of her hand towards him. 'No Panos, I don't want to hear, just go away.'

He stared and scratched his chin, glared at her companions, turned on his heel and disappeared into the bar. Sarah heard Danni snigger. He lowered his menu and looked at her with his captivating dark brown eyes. 'I was very, very wrong about you. May I join your team?'

The next morning, before going out onto the terrace for her breakfast, she spied Petra sitting on a stool leaning against the bar, staring at his half empty bottle of Metaxa brandy, the television flickering with the sound turned down; yet another mind-numbing game show so early in the morning. She knew this would be a favourable opportunity. He jumped at her appearance and anxiously studied her face with a quizzical expression. Having spent the night fishing, it had given him time to mull over her words from the evening before. She sat next to him and he nervously stubbed out his Karelia cigarette and offered her a brandy. She shook her head and held up a Greek identification badge. His eyes widened as she spoke in perfect Greek, 'Petra. I have evidence that two nights ago you took a bribe to use your boat to collect an illegal cargo of drugs and guns.' His face turned pale and she noticed his hand start to shake. 'The Greek authorities have been tracking this cargo and I don't have to tell you what the repercussions are for you.'

He looked around and stared back at her, sweat beginning to appear on his brow. He shook his head and blubbered, 'I did it for the money. I had no idea it was guns and drugs.' He grabbed her hand and pleaded, 'please, do not tell Kelena. I beg you!'

'I have the power to keep your name out of all this.'

He fixed his startled moist eyes on her. 'You would do this for me?'

She nodded. 'Yes. But there's a catch.'

He quickly looked around again and squeezed her hand. 'Anything,' he pleaded.

She pulled her hand away. 'As you know I have been here for only a few days ...'

He nodded 'Yes. Yes. You are very welcome. My wife, she speak very highly of you!'

She tapped the bar with her badge; his eyes following the movement. 'I am very much aware that you are lazy and leave all the hard work to your wife.'

He gestured with his hands and argued, 'but I work hard on the boat, bringing money in with the fish.'

'No Petra, you are lazy. I've been watching Kelena, wearing herself out. This has got to stop!'

She could sense his stubborn, small island mentality working overtime. 'I'm prepared to keep your involvement with the cargo here ...' she patted her chest, 'our secret, on condition you help Kelena around the hotel. She is a good wife but she deserves better than you.'

He raised his hands, his eyes rolling up to the ceiling. 'Of course,' he agreed, lowering his eyes, pleading, 'I'll be a good husband to her. Yes, you are right, she deserves a better husband.' He smiled. 'Petra can be a good man, Miss Sarah.'

'Kelena and I have become friends and we have promised to keep in touch. If I hear that you have gone back to your old ways ...' she tapped the badge again; his eyes following, 'just think of the dishonour to your family name on this island should you go to prison.'

She knew she had struck gold. His body demeanour stiffened, his face dropped and he bowed his head pleading, 'you have my word, *my word!*' He turned to Kelena's shrine and crossed himself, his face dripping with perspiration.

Just then Kelena came from the terrace and hovered with surprise at the door. Sarah smiled. 'Good morning Kelena, Petra and I have just got to know each other. Haven't we Petra?'

He nodded, wiping his face with one of Kelena's clean napkins and hurried across to his wife, taking the tray and scurrying into the kitchen. Kelena stared opened mouth at Sarah who walked past with a smile on her face. Kelena turned and watched her go onto the terrace as Sarah called back over her shoulder, 'Kelena, be a dear and ask Petra to bring my coffee, please!'

Sarah enjoyed her breakfast. She hoped she had helped at least one deserving person on the island, and tried not to smile each time Kelena came to the tables. Kelena kept looking at her with a sense of bemusement, but not saying a word, just shaking her head. When the phone rang Sarah called out to Kelena in the kitchen, 'that will probably be my uncle. May I take it?'

Kelena looked out through the hatch. 'Yes of course, my amazing friend Sarah.' She looked behind into the kitchen, and then back at Sarah, her eyes wide. 'Sarah, he's loading the dishwasher ... it's a miracle!' She gave the sign of the cross and withdrew.

Janus's voice was subdued and concerned. 'My dear Katie, Ricki told me what happened.'

'Well, he shouldn't have done as it would have been in my report. It all worked out fine in the end.'

'No Katie, he was quite right to tell me. I'm aware there is a lot to report but that can wait for your debrief. I think you should come back in now, but first you must pay a visit to Johnnie and tell him that Ricki is being withdrawn and he's on his own from now on. If he doesn't like it, then remind him we have his contact with Podolski hanging over him. You can tell him about the recording if you like. It makes no difference now. Hedge Farm is delighted with the quality, well done. This business of Danni is a surprise but it was just as well. Wonder what his next move is?'

She laughed. 'I don't suppose he's had time to think about it. I'm sure he's delighted not to suck up to that horrible man.'

'Now here's something that will interest you. There was a message waiting for me this morning when I came in, apparently I'm to expect a call from Capitainé Andre Herisson of the French DGSE. Intriguing don't you think? Bye for now.'

She put the receiver down, and pressed the battery - button as Panos coughed behind her. He looked uneasy and she could see a *little boy reporting to his headmistress*. She spoke in Greek, 'come Panos, come and have coffee with me. I'm sorry I was abrupt last evening but yesterday was a very trying day.'

They sat down together. 'I want to report that the container was picked up and taken on the morning ferry.'

'Thank you Panos.'

He leaned forward with a puzzled expression. 'What has come over Petra? He waved me away and said he didn't have time for a drink. He is too busy!'

She tried not to laugh. 'I have no idea, but maybe he has just peeped over the horizon and seen what is coming. The world is changing Panos, and so must he and all those like him; just think about it!'

The island policeman nodded but didn't really understand. But then there was a lot he didn't understand since this young woman arrived on his island.

18

'... *Johnnie's despair*'

Ricki parked the Escort next to Petra's pickup and they remained in the car. There were several fishermen repairing their brightly coloured nets. Sarah watched Petra in admiration. He was hunched over; sitting cross-legged in the middle of what appeared to be a tangled heap of yellow netting, his right hand deftly and poetically flowing with no apparent break in the movement, repairing exactly as witnessed by Odysseus on the island of Ithaca. The scene moved Sarah as surely it hadn't changed for centuries; the colourful repaired nets hanging out to dry in the morning heat, framed against the backdrop of the vivid blue Mediterranean; the island fishermen chatting and comparing last night's catch. They had glanced up with their brooding lined faces at the arrival of an intruder, but their minds remained in deep concentration, lost in their own island world; a world that outsiders wouldn't understand; she felt the desperate desire to return and paint her picture. The overcast sky was a heavy blanket of humidity and Sarah was already drenched in perspiration; the air smelt of salt and tangy seaweed and fish and tar. They eventually left the car after Sarah commented, 'come on, let's get it over with, I can't wait to see Johnnie's face.' She acknowledged Petra's skill with a smile and he nodded shyly back, surprising her by his appreciation. The guard dog had already started barking before the two walked over the rickety wooden bridge. They didn't need to press the bell as Henry appeared and shoved the animal into its kennel. He grunted and gestured at Sarah by flicking his head in the direction

143

of the terrace. She glared. 'I suppose that means Johnnie is on the terrace?' He didn't reply. As they walked up the path Ricki whispered, 'I've got my belongings already packed.' He held her arm and directed her round to where Johnnie was standing under the awning. He was dressed in the usual paint-splattered shorts, his protruding stomach hanging over the waist-band. He was smoking a cigar and staring at a half finished canvas perched on an easel. He turned and gave them a chilly stare. He waved a brush and motioned her to sit. 'Get some beers in Henry.'

Sarah ignored his obvious goading by walking past and taking in the panoramic view; *ignorant moron* went through her mind; she recalled calling him that a couple of nights before up on the cliff edge when listening on the recorder. Ricki sat down and looked at her slim back and wondered what was going through her head. Tantalisingly she promised to meet up again in London with a kiss, but he had snatched it on the beach; maybe he had blown it? Would she want a relationship back home? It could cause a problem as it was strictly frowned upon within the service; maybe one would have to leave and he couldn't expect her to do it. *I will resign*; his mind was racing ahead, *what should I do?* He knew it didn't enter into her way of thinking here on the island; she was on duty and he admired her resolve. He reflected how composed she had appeared over dinner last evening, but the painful memory of the morning was still there; she was more subdued than normal and occasionally her thoughts were not with her companions...

He pulled his wanderings back to the terrace and Johnnie as Sarah turned and moved over to look at his canvas. Johnnie stood back waiting for a hopeful comment, his cigar drooping from his lips. She raised her eyebrows and sat down. Johnnie dropped his brush into a pot with a sense of annoyance, wiping paint off his hands. 'Well,' he growled, 'do you approve?'

Ricki tried not to smile as she replied, 'I'm not saying I don't like it, and then again, I'm not saying I do like it.'

'I'm not asking you to buy it,' he muttered sitting down.

'Good!'

Henry handed bottles of beer round and Sarah offered acidly, 'where I come from, women do not drink beer from bottles thank you.'

Ricki was enjoying her cat and mouse game. She was composed and she was very good at manoeuvring the situation to her advantage.

Johnnie swigged his bottle and stared at her. 'OK, spit it out. Something tells me you're not here on a social visit.'

She slowly and deliberately poured her beer into the glass. 'Do you want the good news, or the bad news first?'

'OK, let's cut the crap ... the bad news?'

'I don't think you could possibly sell that painting.' Ricki bit his lip and tried to avoid her eyes.

Johnnie gave her a curious stare, his face showing irritation at this woman's game. 'That's the bad news? Well, what's the good news then?'

'The good news is, I have been told by London, to relay to you that we are withdrawing from this island. From now on, you're on your own.'

She knew this was what he wanted, but of course he didn't yet know about Podolski. She paused before continuing the game. 'We know about your involvement with Podolski ...'

'Involvement? he gasped. 'The bottle jerked, beer spilling over his stomach giving an interesting brown sheen to the mound of flesh which Sarah found delightfully entertaining.

'What involvement? He only came to look at my paintings. Ask him,' he shouted, pointing at Ricki.

'Mister Podolski has gone, Johnnie.'

'Gone?' The sweat starting to run down his face.

Sarah smiled sweetly. 'Yes. Disappeared! He's done a runner. Is that how you would say in cockney? He won't be coming back Johnnie. You have my word on it.' She looked at Ricki. 'That's right, isn't it Ricki?'

Ricki nodded and repeated. 'He's gone Johnnie, he's done a scarper.'

Johnnie's eyes bulged. 'But he owes me.'

'Money Johnnie?'

She noticed Henry screwing up his face, his scar a vivid mauve. He stared at his boss. His instinct told him his world was about to crumble.

'... money for your contacts in London, and for helping to get the cargo from the boat the other night? You can forget the pay-off, Johnnie.'

His face glowed red, and he wiped the sweat with an oily rag that left an interesting smear of *Verde-green* paint across his face.

She sipped her beer. 'We watched you and Henry help unload Petra's boat the other evening. We were on the cliff opposite. Oh, by the way, an Inspectorul Sergin Dimitri will be paying you a visit later on today. I should listen very carefully to what he has to say. He has plans for you. You've been a naughty boy Johnnie and London is not happy … not happy at all.'

Ricki could see she was relishing the man's misery as she went on. 'So you won't be enjoying the protection Podolski promised, because he's disappeared. He's gone and done a runner, as I believe you cockneys would say. You've blown it and you can stew in your own juice ... you're not getting any more protection from London.'

Ricki picked his moment and disappeared into the house. Johnnie stared after him and demanded, 'Where's he going? And who the hell is,' he waved his hand, 'Inspectorul Sergin when he's about?'

'Well, you'll find out later, and Ricki's gone to fetch his belongings and collect the listening bug from your lounge.'

For one moment she thought Johnnie was going to have a fit. His eyes bulged, his face turned purple and suddenly the blood drained from his face leaving him slumped and drained. Henry crumpled groaning into a chair with his head in his hands.

Just then Henry's wife Rose poked her head from the sliding door and smiled at Sarah. 'Fancy staying for lunch my dear?'

19

'... an evening at the Spiti'

Ricki followed Panos struggling up the steps of the Spiti carrying Ricki's suitcase. Ricki had taken his leave of Ingissi but found saying goodbye to Rose, rather emotional. Coming from the same area in London there was a common affinity between them. He was concerned for her because their stay on the island was ending, their future uncertain; difficult to return to London; memories run deep in those communities. He knew that the visit by Inspectorul Sergin Dimitri, or Danni, would end in tears for her.

The hotel was packed, so Panos had offered his spare room which surprised, but pleased Sarah. She returned to the hotel leaving Ricki sorting out his belongings whilst Panos made a snack and brewed coffee. The two men appeared to be getting on well. Panos had invited Sarah, Ricki and Danni to dine at his Spiti that evening to a *typical Greek meal*, that he, yes he, would cook.

The Business Attaché's office at the embassy had arranged Sarah's flight back to London for the next day. Ricki would be coming the following day and then the whole chapter would be behind her. She hadn't any feedback from Phillip and knew that was the way it should be. She was delighted to have met up again and thrilled for his success and his delightful family. She had been devastated at their parting, but now Ricki seemed to be coming into the equation, she realised Phillip was a reaction to her own unsatisfactory and empty life. Before getting to the hotel she called into a shop on the front and bought several small gifts to take back home. She wanted to give Kelena a memento of their meeting but couldn't find anything suitable and suddenly realised; of course, she already had something special back at the hotel.

After their lunch on the hotel terrace, she made her way down to the sea for her last swim and Ricki said he would join her later. The beach was very busy and she found a space at the far end, well away from where Geraldine and Harold were stretched out on their sun beds under a large red umbrella. They were both engrossed in their magazines and she managed to slip unseen into the warm, beautifully clear water. She headed for the floating pontoon, unusually empty and pulled herself onto the gently swaying platform to lie down and enjoy the peace away from the busy beach. Tomorrow she'll be back in London and the past few days will seem but a dream. Maybe she should take a sabbatical and return to Oxford and submit her dissertation. Have a year away to sort her life out. Oxford was no distance from London and seeing Ricki would be easy and something to look forward to at weekends. Her parents would be thrilled as she knew how disappointed and surprised they were when she took her job in Whitehall. Suddenly the pontoon shook with shouts from two teenagers climbing on board, oblivious to the young woman already relaxing there. They screamed and jumped off, rocking and splashing the pontoon; she shook her head ... always too good to last, time to make a tactical withdrawal. As she swam away she realised she was able to see the southern tip of the island where the sun was touching a dark scar cutting down the cliff face; the rubbish tip! She felt a chill and the memory of that moment came rushing back; Podolski disappearing under the falling black plastic bags, the flies and the rotting smell; she thought of his body still there. She shuddered and turned, swimming quickly to the shore. The pleasure had gone and all she wanted to do was to get back home. She pulled the towel tightly around her shoulders and felt herself shivering although the afternoon was hot. She sat down, hugging herself, staring lost into the sand. She became aware of a shadow moving across her legs and Ricki sat down beside her.

She looked up and he put his arm around her. She rested her head against his shoulder and silently wept, her tears running down his arm. She went to dry them but he stopped her. 'No leave them, they belong to me now.'

It had nearly all ended on this beautiful holiday island.

Later that evening, having packed, she went down into the bar and noticed Petra laying the tables. She smiled to herself and poked her head around the kitchen door. Kelena looked up and gave her usual warm greeting. Sarah handed a package to her and Kelena looked surprised. She opened it to find the gold cross that Sarah had bought in the shop called Byzantino.

Kelena was overwhelmed. She asked, 'do you know the legend of Athina's eye?'

Sarah knew of course but shook her head.

'She can only bring you protection if this is given as a gift. I always hoped that Petra would give one to me, and now you, a stranger, come from a distant land bearing this gift. She has sent you for this purpose. I know in my heart it was meant to be.'

Sarah put it round the woman's neck and pulled her over to a mirror by the door. Kelena wiped her eyes and gave Sarah a warm and long embrace. They both knew they had made a life-time friendship and Sarah felt good, and yes, she knew it was meant to be.

Sarah explained her evening arrangements and Kelena had raised her eyebrows at the invitation. But she commented, 'I think you will be pleasantly surprised.'

She had arranged to meet the two lads at the Zorba bar. She preferred Danni's real name; Sergin Dimitri; *had a poetic roll of the tongue.*

She showered and dressed very carefully as she wished to make an impression. It had been a long time since she had wanted to take such care with her appearance. She approved of the person in the mirror. She was much tanned against the cream dress and she felt very feminine. The cross would have been perfect around her neck; she would have to visit the dealer in Athens again before heading to the airport. *It was what Athina wanted.*

She walked into the bar causing several heads to turn as Kelena came in from the terrace. She paused admiring the English woman and nodding her approval. She knew what she had to do. Looking thoughtful she took Sarah's arm and led her into her office. She pulled open the desk drawer and took out the cross that Sarah had given to her earlier. 'Sarah, would you please wear this tonight ... for me. It would give me great pleasure to see you in it.' She grinned. 'I think it will impress the men!'

Kelena fastened the clasp and they both looked in the mirror; the Greek woman intrigued and puzzled with the eyes becoming more intense, reflecting the colour of the stones, gold-set matching the copper within her hair. 'See what I mean Sarah. My feeling is someone had that in mind when you bought it.'

Sarah nodded, *yes it was a good choice and it was exactly what Athina had in mind.* Now she was ready to impress Ricki ... *and her future?*

The evening hung warm and clear, somehow the Milky Way seemed most magical as a river of fire in the night sky. Sarah felt a sense of romance with the rising moon at play with her new emotions, its shimmering silk reflection casting across the deep night of sea; only the music of Bach, with Anna dancing to her Sarabande missing from the lapping sea. Before meeting the boys she walked in her bare feet across warm sand to the rocks where Ricki had sat that night. He was right, what's the use of moonlight, sounds of gentle sea, and that music, but to be on your own. Gosh, that seemed of another age. She sat for a while thinking about Ricki, or Andrew as she would rather call him and knew she had to be strong about her new feelings. She reluctantly strolled back enjoying the sensuous feel of warm sand through her toes. Slipping on her casuals she continued her relaxed stroll through the unrestrained holiday makers already filling the bars. The two lads were seated outside; heads down, deep in conversation.

Danni had arrived earlier at Johnnie's to find them in a despondent mood. They had been brooding and arguing over Sarah's visit that morning and also Danni's impending visit; he later described Johnnie's face when he declared his true identity, he had savoured the sweet moment. It appeared that Capitainé Andre Herisson had discussed Johnnie with Janus that morning. The outcome: Johnnie to be offered a passage to South Africa and work for the French DGSE as a retired business man. There was a wealth of intelligence to glean from the bars full of mercenaries looking for contracts and people offering blood diamonds. In return he would get a retainer and come under the DGSE protection. Danni also knew that Johnnie wouldn't be returning. He had seen these *strays* before, as he liked to call them. Misfits under the wing of a secret service, placed under so-called protection, out in the old colonies, propping up bars as Graham Green cardboard characters, soaking up intelligence from the flotsam hanging around, hunched over half empty bottles of bourbon and passing snippets of information to their controllers; people wary of them as if they had spy tattooed on the foreheads; they could smell them. Eventually their livers succumb to the drink and their final resting place positioned in an out of town cemetery attended by a priest and maybe his only friend, the barman; maybe a man dressed in a suit from the embassy; his controller standing out of sight in the shade, paying his last respects before welcoming a new recruit to the bar. That was to be Johnnie's future and it was an offer he couldn't really refuse; the alternative being a return to London and serve out his sentence; old friends in London wanting to meet up again and settle their scores. Rose had put her foot down and insisted on returning to London; in the end, a reluctant Henry agreeing to return with her.

Sarah appeared unnoticed at their table and coughed. They both looked up, and yes, they were impressed. Years later she would often recall the look on Ricki's face, and that's when she knew she had to make up her mind about her future; or lose him.

Panos's anxious face peered round the door at his three grinning guests. They were very surprised with the care he had taken in laying the table. It was obvious he had gone to a great deal of trouble to make the evening a success. He wore a blue-striped chef's apron with *Beachcomber* across the front. Nothing was said, but they did wonder about the curious fifth setting. Sergin became intrigued with the library and spent time looking through the collection. Panos kept glancing at his watch and suddenly dashed into the kitchen, reappearing and giving handwritten menu cards to his amused and hungry guests. He watched their faces for approval, scratching his chin:

CAFE PANOS
Starter — Pantzária Saláta
(Beetroot salad with garlic sauce)
Main course — Tás Kebáb
(Pork and peppers in tomato sauce, served with rice)
Desert — Glyká
(Sweets)
Hálvá
(Cake made with semolina)
Mythos
(Wine)

They glanced to Panos with his reaction from the sudden and unsure tapping on the door, and much to the amusement of his guests, showing signs of panic, tearing off the apron and throwing it wildly through the kitchen doorway. He looked in the mirror, brushing his hair, straightening his collar and hesitantly opening the door. They watched, staring in anticipation ... who was the other guest?

She peered shyly around the door. Ricki was the first to whisper, 'why, it's Marilyn Monroe.' The young blond, unsure of her reception, stood hovering and watching the faces as Panos kissed her cheek. He turned beaming. 'I believe you have seen Denise before.' Sarah and Ricki tried not to grin and they all shook hands. Sergin took her hand and as he kissed it he caught Sarah's eye, daring him to quote Shakespeare. He smiled, shrugged his shoulders and didn't say a word. Panos fussed and they waited for her high-pitched giggle but it remained silent. She sat next to Sarah who warmed to her during the evening; she certainly wasn't the girl she had expected. Once she whispered to Sarah, 'I used to have a giggle because I was told that men found it very attractive, until Panos told me it drove him up the wall.' She fluttered her long false eyelashes at Panos sitting on the other side of the table. 'I spent weeks practicing it back at the office. Thinking about it,' she smiled, 'I think they were pleased when I left for my holiday.'

Ricki piped up, 'Oh that's a shame because I think it's very alluring.' Panos glared at him and Sarah discretely kicked his leg. During the dinner Sarah noticed Ricki admiring the pendant around her neck. On one occasion, he noticed her looking and he nodded his approval that she found pleasurable.

Kelena was right; Sarah was impressed with his cooking and the way he presented the meal. It turned out he originally trained as a chef on leaving school and worked in Athens until his national service. She felt a sadness at leaving the island. It was unusual on an assignment to make friends … and this was her last night. Sarah asked Denise when her holiday was finishing. She blushed, glancing at Panos. He took her hand. 'Denise is staying here with me. She's not going back.'

After the stunned silence, Ricki leaned over and whispered in Sarah's ear, 'this will be a learning curve for her.' Sarah grinned as Denise looked at Panos and tapping the table she announced, 'I'm going to look after him and starting tomorrow, Panos is going on a diet.' The evening ended as laughter filled the Spiti and Sarah murmuring to Ricki, 'a learning curve for them both I think.'

After they had said their goodnights, Ricki walked her slowly to the Mira. He was intrigued by the *Athina Eye* around her neck, so she confessed she had first bought it for herself, but decided to give it to Kelena who had asked her to wear it especially for him that evening.

As they neared the hotel she stopped and asked, 'Andy, early tomorrow morning would you come with me to the Chapel of Santa Maria please, I don't want to go on my own.'

He nodded. 'Yes of course. I would love to.'

She suddenly put her arms around him. 'Thank you. I'm saving mine for London, but this is from Athina,' and kissed him goodnight.

Early the next morning, the sun had just lifted off the horizon as Sarah pushed open the heavy and weathered pine door to enter the Santa Maria Chapel that seemed to hover precariously on the cliff edge; looking down on the town of Petromos as it had done for centuries. The squeaking door disturbed an elderly woman dressed head to toe in black, sitting near the shrine of Maria. She looked up from her devotion, crossed herself and rose to leave.

Sarah apologised to her in Greek but the islander's lined and blessed face smiled, indicating that she was just leaving and headed for the door. She then tried to quietly close the squeaking door behind her, leaving the two strangers from another land.

The small chapel held a musty coolness from the morning warmth outside. A few simple wooden chairs faced the silver-framed icon of Maria; from the apex of the roof, a shaft of sunlight streamed through clear ancient glass onto the rear wall, casting distorted rays to scatter as rainbow colours playing across obscure hidden stones, worn shiny from centuries of homage.

Sarah knelt whilst Ricki remained at the rear of the tiny Chapel to watch the woman who was unexpectedly changing his life; he felt moved by her sincerity and desire to share her private moment with him. She rose and lit two candles alongside the single candle left earlier by the woman in black.

She turned and came to put her arm through his. 'Thank you, Andy. I couldn't leave this island without lighting a candle for Ion and Podolski. They weren't born evil; the world made them the way they were. It is us who should ask forgiveness.'

Ricki opened the door and they left the candles to burn out in their own time.

'... each long goodbye, 'tis forever short'

They breakfasted together and before collecting her luggage, Sarah borrowed scissors from Kelena to cut a twig from the olive tree; one more important gesture before leaving her Greece. This time she found saying her goodbyes very difficult. Kelena wanted to come down to the quay, but Sarah knew it would make matters worse, so they said goodbye in the office away from the other guests. Kelena was excited and exclaimed, 'I don't know what you said to Petra but he has changed. I'm getting all those jobs done that I've been nagging about for years, even that dripping gutter outside your bedroom.'

Sarah grinned and replied, 'the power of prayer Kelena.'

Kelena suddenly looked inquisitively and asked, 'where were you born Sarah?'

She hesitated. 'I was born here in Athens, did you not guess? Also my grand mamma was born in Athens.'

Kelena nodded. 'Of course, I should have known because you have Athina's eyes. It has puzzled me since we first met. I understand all now, how foolish of me. I'm convinced you will return.'

Geraldine and Harold said their goodbyes before going off for their final swim before catching the afternoon ferry to go home. Even Petra came over and they clumsily embraced; her last image of the couple waving goodbye with Petra holding his astonished wife's arm.

Ricki helped carry her luggage down to the quay where Sergin and Panos waited. Marilyn Monroe stood on the top step of the Spiti waving to Sarah before turning, disappearing inside to prepare their salad lunch and grape juice. Sarah pulled Sergin to one side and asked him about the contact that Podolski reckoned he had in London. 'That's been taken care of,' he replied, trying to change the subject.

She wouldn't let it go. 'Who is it?'

Sergin remained silent and lit a cigarette, weighing up his answer. 'That was part of the discussion Capitainé Herisson had with your Janus.'

She stared at him. 'Well? What happened?'

He puffed out one of his smoke rings. 'Janus should be telling you this.'

'Well he's not here and I want to know!'

'Apparently their conversation got a bit heated because Janus realised that somebody was reporting to Capitainé Herisson.'

Sarah glared. 'He had a spy in our office? Great! I thought we were on the same side.'

Sergin laughed. 'He agreed to withdraw his man on condition Janus withdraw his from the DGSE.'

Sarah's eyes widened. 'We had someone in the DGSE?'

Sergin nodded and shrugged his shoulders. 'Fair enough, don't you think?'

She shook her head and Sergin commented, 'it's all a game of chess Sarah; you take my King so I take your Queen, and we go round and round in circles till the next time.'

'No wonder I'm getting out.'

He frowned. '*Out*, no you mustn't get out!'

'Only a few hours ago you told me to go home and have a family.'

He held his hands up. 'I did apologise. I was wrong. I'm sorry.'

'No Sergin, you were right. That is precisely what I want to do. Anyway, I never could get my head around political chess.' Suddenly the crazy thought entered her head ... *political chess ... Major Bentley-Snade ... Janus not trusting him; surely not!*

Just then, they became aware of the ferry's arrival with the sudden blast from its siren bouncing around the bay, the bow door already starting to lower. Sergin leaned forward and kissed her hand. 'Goodbye Sarah, I hope to see you in London before I take Johnnie down to South Africa.' He then withdrew leaving Ricki and Sarah alone.

Sarah felt weary; the hour-long journey back to Piraeus seemed to go on forever with the screaming kids running across the decks: Her side still tender as she struggled through the mass of people trying to disembark from the *Hellas Athina* in one piece. The dock compound was hot and dirty. Piraeus now busy with its noisy rush-hour traffic; the smell of diesel hung in the air.

Suddenly behind her, a voice called out, 'Miss Simpson?' She swung round and looked into the enquiring face of a smart uniformed chauffeur. She recognised him as the embassy driver, Tommy. His ex-military bearing and manner she found reassuring; seemingly standing to attention as he touched his cap, looking her up and down.

'I've come to take you to the Embassy Miss and you have a parcel for security I believe.' His voice clipped and to the point.

She reached for the parcel, with the bible, to go back to London in the Diplomatic pouch. She looked for the security agent who should have been with the car, but Tommy made a facial gesture.

'It's OK, you can hand it in yourself as I've instructions to take you to the Business Attaché's office. He grabbed her bag and marched towards the black Mercedes parked within the ferry compound.

Sarah paused and shouted at his back. 'I have to get to the airport and I need to do some shopping before leaving Athens … and why the office … and where is security?'

He opened the car boot shrugging his shoulders. 'Orders are orders Miss. Apparently, you are now catching the later flight. I'll be taking you to the airport so you'll have plenty of time.'

She gratefully settled into the welcome, air-conditioned coolness of the Mercedes as it whisked through the traffic, thankful to be away from the outside heat and bustle of Athens but annoyed with yet another change of plan. Her mind started racing, trying to think why she had to return to the Embassy. She became aware of his eyes in the mirror.

Been on holiday, miss?'

'Yes, something like that.'

'Better than driving through this traffic every day, miss.' He turned through the gate security into the familiar Embassy compound and pointed at a temporary portacabin near the entrance. 'You have to take your parcel in there miss, it's all changing I'm afraid.'

She tutted, walked across and tapped on the door. Nothing happened. She was already irritated and tapped again, but louder. A voice commanded, 'Come in'.

She opened the door and entered. A young man was staring at a monitor, he muttered over his shoulder, 'won't keep you long.'

Her eyes glared and she snapped, 'What did you say? Look at me when you speak to me!' She demanded.

He turned and stared. He was in his early twenties, pale skinned, washy eyes and a weak chin, his lanky hair reaching his collar.

She stared back appalled, thinking, *God; they're recruiting straight from school.*

'Your name please?' he asked coldly.

'Are you supposed to be security?' she sniped back. 'Why didn't you meet me at Piraeus?' She was fuming.

'Are you Miss Athina-Beaumont?' he asked.

'You know damn well I am, so what's all this about?'

'It was pointless coming as you've been summoned to the Business Attaché's office.'

Her hackles rose. 'Nobody summons me young man. Now take this parcel,' she demanded, sharply pushing it across the desk. He opened a drawer and pulled out a pad. He placed it in front of her, putting a pen next to it. 'You need to fill this in and sign at the bottom,' he said turning back to the monitor.

She flipped over the two-page questionnaire; ignoring the column of questions, she scrawled her signature across the bottom and threw the pad back across the desk with the pen. 'Fill the damn thing in yourself.' He turned back to her; she stared at his identity tag hanging from his neck, looking like a wartime evacuee. 'Well Clive Stamford-Montfort, I'll remember that name because next year when you visit Hedge Farm for your annual refresher, I'll probably be your instructor and you'll wish you hadn't been born.' As she started to storm out she shouted back, 'and get that hair cut before we meet again.' Deliberately leaving the cabin door wide open, she strode back to the car, shaking.

'Tommy, can I sit in your car, I need to calm down?'

Tommy studied her face and smiled. 'He's only been here a month ... they learn in the end. They're all the same miss, straight from school.' He opened the door and she flopped into the cool interior.

'Damn bureaucracy,' she shouted. 'Is this what they're now recruiting? Heaven help us.' She so wanted to share a moan with Ricki. She suddenly started to giggle aloud with a form of relief after the past few days. She wiped her eyes. 'Gosh, I enjoyed that. Just what I needed, perhaps he did me a favour? Wait until I tell Ricki, or Andrew, or is it Andy? Heaven help us all.' She laughed out loud.

A few minutes later a curious Tommy tapped the window pointing at his watch. Having calmed down she adjusted her hair and retouched her lipstick. Outside the car, she straightened her blouse and brushed away the creases from her skirt. 'Well Tommy, will I do?' she asked.

He grinned, sharply looking her up and down with approval. 'You look very nice to me miss. In fact, you'll do nicely.'

She entered into the cool and quiet marbled reception hall of the British Embassy. A young, attentive Greek girl rose up from behind her desk and asked, 'Miss Simpson?' Sarah nodded and the girl said, 'you are expected in the Business Attaché's office.' She made a gesture of showing her the direction, but Sarah nodded. 'Thank you, I do know the way.' She headed for the sweeping marble staircase; she always found the effort of trying to walk quietly up those wide marble steps somehow intimidating; trying not to be awed by their classical beauty.

She paused at the heavy mahogany door, at first touching the gleaming *Business Attaché* brass plate with her fingers. Taking a deep breath, she muttered angrily to herself, 'summoned ... damn cheek!' She clenched her hand into a fist and knocked. The door sharply opened, her heart skipped a beat as she looked into his warm dark eyes ...

'Hello once again, Katie Simpson.'

'... the end doth her beginning make'

She looked stunned and gasped, 'Phillip!'

He took her arm and kissed her on the cheek. He led her into the high, ornate ceiling room where a woman waited that Katie recognised from the photograph. His two small children stood shyly clutching their mother. 'Katie I would like you to meet Elissa.' He noticed what appeared to be to be a difficult pause as Elissa studied the woman before her ... those eyes; of course Katie was an Athinian woman, she then understood it all. Elissa suddenly hugged Katie.

'Katie I've heard so much about you since Phillip came back from the island, and so I demanded to meet the other woman in his life.'

Katie felt herself blush and looked awkwardly at Phillip. 'Oh dear,' she murmured.

Elissa laughed. 'I'm only teasing.' She turned to the children. 'This is Jerome and this is Helen.'

Katie crouched and gave the shy children a tight cuddle.

Lighting a cigarette, Phillip leaned against the green veined marble fireplace with its cherub reliefs dominating the room, quietly observing the two women warmly chatting. They were sitting on the damask window seat that followed the gentle curve of the Gaussian window, the distant hum of Athen's morning traffic droning in the background. Helen stood leaning against her mother, looking intently at the stranger; Jerome hurried away and sat in the huge office chair behind the desk, swivelling backwards and forward.

Phillip studied Katie. She seemed so different to the woman he briefly met on the island. She looked tense when he first opened the door, but now relaxed and looking happy – yes, she looked happy. He had been worried since that rumour had circulated about her being involved in something bad on the island. He had wondered if this meeting was such a good idea. Elissa was aware he seemed subdued after coming back from his sudden visit to Petromos; he had been distant, seemingly worried, and so one morning she gently raised the subject. Of course, she had known about Katie and Michael from his youth, he would often talk warmly of those times, but suddenly she had reappeared back into his life. This meeting was her idea; she wanted him to confront this shadow. She was right of course; this shadow from his past was clinging to an illusion that the Phillip of today was the same Phillip of her youth. He had moved on but Katie had been so involved in her busy career, she had become trapped in her distant memories. Elissa wanted Katie to see Phillip in his adult life, with his family around him. Now she was here, and the two women of important diverse times in his life were getting on so well - *she does look good!* At one point he became aware they both were staring at him and grinning. *Oh dear, what are those two women confiding?* he wondered.

Suddenly Elissa looked at her watch. 'Phillip, I must go and do that shopping, and Katie has a plane to catch.' They stood up and she continued, 'I will take the children and leave you two here on your own, I think you both have a lot to talk about. I'll see you outside Phillip, and then Katie must hurry off to the airport.' She turned and the two women hugged. 'Remember Katie, whenever you come to Athens you must promise to come and see us. Promise?'

A tearful Katie nodded and watched as Phillip's family took their leave; the young girl whispering, 'who is that lady mummy?' and the young boy, protesting, wanting to stay with his father and continue to swivel in the large chair.

Phillip took her arm and they both sat down on the window seat as he wiped her wet cheek with his hand; she was looking out of the window lost in thought. She suddenly smiled at him and started gushing. 'Oh Phillip, Elissa is so nice and your two children ... I didn't think I'd ever see you again and in many ways I thought it would be for the best ... but now I'm glad because I can see how happy you are ... and I was carried away on Petromos ... and I acted like a silly young girl—'

Phillip broke into the excited flow. 'Sorry about the surprise but it was Elissa's idea to meet up again. She obviously understood what you were feeling and I suppose she hoped a meeting with you would clear the air ... I wasn't sure that it was a good idea, but of course she was right. When I left you I was very worried and then I heard you were involved in some ... incident and ... you do look so happy Katie?'

She explained about Ricki and her decision to withdraw from fieldwork and concentrate on getting her personal life back together. 'It was our meeting up again, I realised I had sacrificed those years for the department ... and it all nearly ended on the island. A Romanian there told me to go home and have a family. At first, he made me angry, but he was right ...' She smiled at him, '... and here I am, hopefully heading back home to a new life. And I've met your lovely family, and yes, I feel hopeful!'

'I'm sorry, I forgot to ask about your wound?'

'It's fine Phillip. I had a wonderful doctor.'

He laughed. 'Yes, and you have Ricki. I get the feeling he's your best medicine.'

As they walked down the long flight of stairs to the reception area, Katie put her arm through his and the young Greek girl smiled and said goodbye. Tommy sat in the corner reading his paper and jumped up smartly at their appearance. He followed them out into the heat of the day and opened the rear door for her. He watched the Embassy Doctor and his passenger embrace and kiss, and as she sat in the car, Phillip leaned in and said, 'don't forget to send us the wedding invite.' She frowned. 'Don't rush me

Phillip ... people can be so different back in a grey London.

He handed her a folded slip of paper. 'Maybe this will help. Do you remember I had this paper with Ricki's description of a certain Sarah Athina-Beaumont he gave the Embassy when we first met at the jetty?'

She hesitantly stared at the folded paper.

He watched the car pull away and turn from Ploutarchou Street into the Odos Vasilissis Sofias, and then felt Elissa's arm tight around him. She smiled. 'She is so nice Phillip. I like her. I can now understand your warm memories together.'

'How long have you been here?'

'Not long.'

'You didn't go shopping did you?'

She shook her head. 'We went for a walk in the park. I felt you both should be alone; I would have done in Katie's shoes.' As they walked round to where their car was parked, she commented, 'I know you were both children at the time, but I'm glad she ran away when you tried to kiss her, she couldn't possibly let you of course because her life was planned from when she was born; I read it in her eyes; only Athinian women can recognise that look. But I think she is now free. She too realises her bond is now released and that is why she looks so happy. I'm glad it wasn't me that was chosen. And of course, my life would have been completely different if she hadn't run away, and so would have yours!'

He stopped and turned to stare at her, puzzled. 'Would you repeat that, it's difficult to follow. And what's this you say ... bond? And who told you about the kiss?'

She grinned. 'Women's talk.' She pulled at his arm. 'Come on Philip Makris lets go home ... you may be a doctor but you men have such a lot to learn.'

In the car Katie leaned forward to Tommy. 'Before we go to the airport I want to go to Plaka. Have we still time?'

He nodded. Cutting across the busy lanes he headed towards

the Acropolis district. She opened the note, raising her eyebrows as she read the scribbled words and then she kissed the writing. He eventually pulled in to double-park outside the Byzantino jewellery shop. She said, 'I shan't be long, if you have to move I'll wait for you.'

He looked at her in the mirror. 'No problem. Be as long as you like as we have plenty of time. This is an Embassy car the police won't take any notice.'

She once again entered her favourite shop in Athens but not before noticing the "*closing down*" sign in the art gallery window. Inside Byzantino were several tourists admiring the jewellery displays, and the young girl who had served her several days before looked up. She showed recognition and came over.

'Miss Simpson?'

Katie looked surprised as the girl moved to a set of wooden drawers taking out a box that she placed on the glass counter. 'I believe this is what you have come for?' She watched Katie's expression as she lifted out a gold cross pendant with Athina's eye similar to the one that she had bought several days before and now left with Kelena.

Katie hesitated. 'I don't understand. Yes, I came to buy a replacement as I gave the other one to a friend. How did you know?'

'I had a telephone call this morning, and the gentleman explained and tried to describe the cross to me.' She giggled. 'His description was funny.' The girl continued, 'I knew which one, and I remember you trying it on when you bought it. You looked so nice. Each one is individually made and they all vary slightly. I don't know why, but somehow I knew you would be back and so I kept this perfect one for you. It expresses the same sentiment … it's paid for, and importantly he wanted you to know that it's a *gift* … you would understand.'

Katie didn't quite know what to say, she swallowed and nodded. 'It's lovely. Did he leave his name?' She didn't have to ask the girl of course, but so needed the girl to say it.

The girl looked at the piece of paper. 'Andrew. He sounded very nice. He must be very fond of you to buy this!'

Katie nodded. 'Yes. I think he is. But I wasn't sure whether I would have time to call in.'

'Would you like to wear it now?'

'Yes please. I would like that very much.'

As the girl fitted the clasp together, Katie admired the mirror image; the central stone reflecting her own deep slate-green eyes ... *she will be pleased.* She asked, 'supposing I hadn't come in?'

'He gave me his number and said that I was to ring him back if you didn't come, he would collect it on his way through tomorrow. Oh yes.' The girl blushed. 'He asked me to write this down for you.'

Katie stared at the message; her eyes widened and read it twice. The girl shyly looked away, asking, 'would you like to keep it?'

Katie nodded and put it in her blouse pocket together with the other note. As she made to leave the shop she paused at the door, deep in thought, fingering the pendant round her neck; the Eye burning against her skin, *...come on Katie, not this time ... don't push him away as you've always done to the others ... don't be a fool yet again ... you know this is her wish for you ... the meeting with Philip and Andrew ... she had it planned all along.* She smiled at the girl. 'Would you ring him back and tell him ... that's how I feel about him ... and the answer is *Yes!*'

The dew-eyed go-between reached for the phone and dialled, taking her straight to the island of Petromos with Katie's reply.

Katie sat in the Mercedes feeling the small sprig of olive tree in her bag. Before heading back to London, she had to give her thanks to Athina with what she knew would, sadly, be their final goodbye.

She leaned forward. 'Tommy, first I have to visit the Parthenon. I have something of importance to do ...'